An Endless Dawn

An Endless Dawn

Avril Sabine

Cracked Acorn Productions
Australia

An Endless Dawn

Published by

Cracked Acorn Productions

PO Box 1365

Gympie, Queensland 4570

Australia

978-1-925617-16-0 (Kindle)

978-1-925617-17-7 (EPUB)

978-1-925617-18-4 (Print)

Genre: Post Apocalyptic Sci-Fi

Cover design by Caitlyn Petersen

For those friends who no matter how much time has passed, it only seems like minutes since we were last together.

The beginning of a new dawn.

When an alien life form is discovered and brought back to Earth, the possibilities seem endless. Piper is fascinated from the beginning, wanting to know everything about the plant and desperate to own one when a limited amount are released to the public. There are of course the usual rumours and crazy people who preach that the end of the world is coming. But Piper knows better. It's the most monumental discovery and somehow she'll become part of it.

*

This story was written by an Australian author using Australian spelling.

Chapter One

Piper scrolled down the page of her online, private journal. She paused to reread some of the news headlines she knew off by heart. 'A New Dawn for Man.' 'Could this be the First Step in Proving the Existence of Aliens?' 'Experiments Begun on Dawn in Sterile Environment.' 'Dawn Laboratory Sabotaged.' 'Discovery of the Century: Will Pollution be a Fear of the Past?'

She stared longer at her two favourite headlines. 'Propagation of Dawn Proven Successful.' 'Seedlings Available for the Public to Purchase Soon.' She remembered the moment she'd first read them and the thrill that had raced through her. Now she had a new favourite headline.

Reaching the bottom of the page, she pasted in the latest article. She stared at the image of the vividly green plant with its dainty leaves. Her gaze was drawn to the headline above the image. 'Dawn Available in Selected Shops Tomorrow.' Her heart leapt again as she reread the words. She'd been waiting for this moment for what felt like forever. Now if only she could convince her parents to lend her the money. She'd been saving ever since she'd learned it was going to be possible to buy a plant. It was a pity they were so expensive, but she guessed it was to be expected since stock was limited and being sold worldwide. She didn't have two thousand dollars for a seedling. Somehow she had to make her parents understand how important this was to her.

Her gaze was drawn to her bedroom door, but she remained seated at her desk. They were probably in the living room, watching the news. She doubted they'd spend that much money on her, but what else could she do? This was important. She had to make them understand. She tried to think of ways to approach them, going so far as to whisper a few sentences. Nothing sounded right. All she could do was try. Rising from her desk, she strode to her bedroom door. She paused, a smile starting to form.

Maybe she could remind them it was discovered by someone from their country. The astronaut might have been born in China, but he'd moved to Australia as a child so that made it an Australian discovery.

They could argue back and forth on the news about which country the discovery belonged to, but it was here in Australia, even though most of the companies now involved were foreign. She headed for the living room, trying to think of more reasons why they had to buy her a plant.

Her parents, Alistair and Tricia, were seated together watching the news that was displayed on the far wall of their small living room. They both had ordinary brown hair that they'd passed along to her. Alistair's hair was thinning while Tricia's fell around her shoulders, almost as long as her own. They looked up at her where she stood in the doorway and she met her mum's blue eyes first before shifting her gaze to meet her dad's green eyes, identical to hers.

"Is something wrong?" Alistair asked.

She shook her head, settling on a plan. Well, something of a plan. She'd ease into the topic and remind them of how much it meant to her. Remind them that it would be almost unpatriotic not to be involved. "Have you seen the news? About Dawn."

"It'd be a little hard to miss," Alistair said dryly.

"I've heard it constantly for the past couple of hours," Tricia said. "It's on every station. Surely there's more important news."

Obviously her plan wasn't going exactly the way she'd expected. "Don't you think it's awesome?"

"What would be more awesome was if we didn't have to hear about Dawn half a dozen times a day," Tricia said.

Alistair chuckled. "And not only from the news." He shared a look with Tricia, who smiled at him.

Piper's heart sank. Didn't they understand how important this was? "It's the greatest moment since man walked on the moon and our country was the one that discovered Dawn. I doubt anyone alive remembers that space event."

"I'm sure some people are alive," Tricia said.

"Babies don't count. They wouldn't have been old enough to realise how important walking on the moon was."

"There've been other great events," Alistair said.

Piper shook her head. "Not this amazing and not space related."

"What about the Mars colonisation project?" Tricia asked.

"That doesn't count. It was a failure. Dawn would have changed all that. She would have made the environment more suitable so the project wouldn't have failed." She'd heard there were plans to take Dawn on the next Mars mission. There'd been nothing in the news, only rumours. She knew, because she'd been scouring the news sites ever since she'd heard the rumour.

"Is there a reason you're telling us something we already know?" Tricia asked.

It looked like easing into it wasn't going to work. "I really need one. This is the most monumental thing that will ever happen in my lifetime and I want to be a part of it." She needed to be a part of it. "And it'd be unpatriotic not to be."

Alistair shook his head. "We can't afford two thousand dollars. You'll have to wait until prices come down. I'm sure they will, particularly since the plant grows fast in polluted environments. You'll probably end up getting a cutting for free."

She spoke quickly, not wanting to get him started on the topic of pollution. Then she'd never have a chance to convince them. "That's too long a wait. I've got three hundred and seven dollars I can put towards it. Mum, Dad, please?" She drew the last word out, mentally begging them as her gaze shifted from one to the other.

"You can plead all you want, it's not going to change facts. We can't afford it," Alistair said.

"But-"

"Didn't you hear me? We can't afford it. There are

too many bills to deal with at this time of year. Maybe by your seventeenth birthday we can buy you one."

Her heart sank. That was ages away. Four entire months. A third of a year. How was she meant to wait that long? Her shoulders slumped. "I'm going next door." She didn't bother saying goodbye as she headed for the door. How could they have said no? They should know how important this was to her. It was all she'd talked about since Dawn was discovered.

"Be back before dinner," Tricia called after her.

She stepped into the corridor of the apartment building, letting the door close behind her. Why couldn't they understand? She'd devoured every bit of news about Dawn since the moment the plant had been discovered and brought back to Earth in a glass container. Those first images were burned into her brain and she could see them as clearly as if the images were currently in front of her. Which wasn't surprising with the amount of times she'd stared at them.

Reaching the elevator she addressed the control panel. "Ground floor." While she waited for the elevator, she continued to think about the many images she'd seen. The next lot of photos the world had been shown was of the lab where testing had been carried out. An artificial environment of glass and stainless steel filled with people in white coats. Her first glimpse of the small piece of plant being studied had caused excitement to race through her. It had immediately been followed by envy that she wasn't old enough to be one of the scientists privileged to work on the Dawn Project. The elevator arrived and she entered, waiting for it to reach the ground floor.

There had to be some way for her to get her own plant. Maybe she should have let her dad get started on his favourite rant. The plant thrived on pollution, cleaning toxins from the air, releasing oxygen back into it. Her dad had said often enough that people needed to do more about pollution. That if they kept going the way they were there'd be no Earth left for future generations. He'd gone on about it so many times she'd long since stopped listening to him. But if being bored for a couple of hours was what it took to get her own plant then maybe she should have let him ramble on about his numerous complaints over the state of the world. People had been predicting the destruction of the planet forever and it obviously hadn't happened.

The elevator door slid open and she stepped outside, crossing the foyer. Before she'd reached the exit, she sent a message to Selene, her best friend, with her communication device to tell her she was on the way over. A reply came back almost immediately.

Will meet you out the front.

She stared at the words for a moment. It had only been an hour since she'd seen Selene at school so she shouldn't have any news she didn't want her mother to overhear. Which was the only reason Selene ever wanted to meet outside.

Piper had nearly reached the front door of Selene's apartment building when her friend burst outside, hurrying towards her. She smiled in greeting, not bothering to walk any faster. The smile had been more than enough effort. All she could think about was how to get her own Dawn. There had to be a way. Over and over she came up with and discarded ridiculous ideas. The situation was hopeless, but the thought of giving up made her feel ill. She had to be a part of the first release of Dawn.

Selene's black hair was pulled up in a short ponytail that bounced with her movements, her dark brown eyes gleaming with excitement. "I was about to send you a message when yours came through."

"What about?"

"That I was coming over to see you and could you meet me out here."

She really hoped Selene wasn't going to expect her

to get excited about her news. She doubted she'd be able to manage. "Are you going to tell me or do I need to drag every little detail out of you?"

Selene grabbed hold of her hands, squeezing tightly as she shook them. "I'm getting one."

Piper frowned. "Getting one what?"

"A Dawn. Mum said it'd be my birthday and Christmas presents all in one and I better not expect anything else this year. And I don't have to wait the six weeks until my birthday. I'm getting it tomorrow." Selene barely paused for breath. "Do you want to come with me?"

"Go with you? Tomorrow?" A moment of jealousy struck before it was replaced by excitement. She grinned. "You're so lucky. I'll ask my parents if I can go." She started to draw away from Selene, alternating between excitement and jealousy. She was thrilled for her friend but she desperately wanted a plant of her own.

Selene's grip tightened and she shook her head. "No, tonight. Apparently people are already lining up at the shops. I'm supposed to go straight home once I've asked you. I need to help Mum organise everything. We're staying the entire night. Do you think you'll be able to come?"

Chapter Two

For a moment words failed Piper as goosebumps rose on her arms. This was what she'd wanted. To be a part of it. To experience every little step of Dawn's journey on Earth. "All night? Right through until the shop opens?"

"Yes." Selene's ponytail bounced energetically in time with her head.

Piper wanted to squeal in excitement. But she couldn't. She had to focus. Her parents might be difficult to convince. "I'll ask. I won't be long." She pulled away from Selene and ran back inside to the elevator. "Floor twenty-two." Her foot tapped as she waited for it to arrive. When it did, she nearly barrelled into one of the tenants, muttering an apology at the glare she received. When the elevator door finally opened again, she raced to the door of her apartment, letting it slam shut behind her, coming to a skidding stop in the living area.

"What's wrong?" Alistair was on his feet before she'd stopped.

"Nothing." She took a deep breath, trying to calm her racing heart. "Selene is getting a Dawn and they're going to line up tonight so they don't miss out. Her mum said I can go too. Can I?" She'd spoken so quickly the words tumbled out all over each other.

"Slow down," Alistair said. "Now start again."

She took another deep breath trying to speak slower. She was afraid if they took too long to decide Selene wouldn't be there in time to buy a plant. Repeating her earlier words, she bit back the demand she wanted to make. Telling them to hurry up and say yes wouldn't give her the outcome she wanted. Her parents were full of questions. They asked about who else would be there, what they planned to do for dinner and what time she'd be home tomorrow. All she could think about was that Selene might let her have a cutting of her Dawn when it grew big enough. Unable to answer a single question, Piper suggested they talk to Selene's mum and they headed to the apartment building, next door, to speak to Evelyn.

While the adults talked, Piper helped Selene put

retro fold up chairs, blankets, food and drinks in Evelyn's vehicle as they waited for a verdict. They were about to head back to the apartment when their parents entered the underground parking garage.

Piper held her breath, almost afraid to ask what their decision was. She clasped her hands together in an effort not to grab hold of them and beg them to say yes. "Well? Can I go?"

Her parents nodded and she squealed, bouncing up and down excitedly with Selene, the warnings and rules unintelligible noises in the background. She was going to be a part of it. The plant might not be hers, but at least she'd be there, at Selene's side as she bought one. And she'd be able to visit Selene every day and watch Dawn's progress. It was the next best thing to having her own plant. Not that she was going to give up on finding a way to own a Dawn.

When they arrived at the shopping complex, the queue went halfway down the block, many of the shops in the complex having remained open to take advantage of the crowds drawn by the coming sale of the seedlings. They set up their chairs at the end of the line, draping blankets over the back of them for later in the night. Piper couldn't stop grinning. There was a hum of excitement in the air as people talked and laughed and children played nearby. There were all kinds of people in the line. Young, old and even babies in prams. It was late afternoon, the sun a glow in the sky. They had a long night ahead of them, but Piper didn't mind. This was what she'd wanted. To be here at the start and to help nurture some of the first seedlings, watching them grow in their new environment. It would be the first time Dawn had been taken out of the sterile stainless steel and glass environment of the lab. The plants were going to be in the real world, not some artificial place created by scientists. Even the natural environment, Dawn had at one stage been tested in, had been created by scientists. Excitement ran through her, like electricity, making it difficult to sit still.

Several metres ahead of them an argument broke out and Piper tried to see around the people in front of her. When those in front also leaned out to see what was happening, she had to lean further. The chair started to feel like it might close up on her.

"Take your propaganda somewhere else."

She watched as a man threw a scrunched up piece of paper at a young man holding a stack of flyers.

Selene leaned close to Piper. "Can you see what's happening?"

She debated telling Selene not to lean against her chair. She didn't want to end up on the ground.

"Some idiot has a pile of old-fashioned flyers. I'm surprised more people haven't complained about wasting our natural resources to print advertisements." She watched the young man move onto the next person who was shaking their head and holding up a hand as if to ward him off.

"I wonder what it says." Selene continued to lean across Piper.

"It looks like we're about to find out." Piper pushed Selene out of the way as the young man stopped in front of them, holding out a flyer. He wasn't much older than her. His sandy brown hair was a few shades lighter than her brown hair. It was short and messy, like he'd run his hands through it repeatedly. She wouldn't have been surprised if he had been doing that going by people's reactions to him.

"Learn the truth." His hazel eyes met hers.

"What truth?" She dragged her gaze from his face to see an image of Dawn on the flyer.

"Here."

She automatically took the flyer. For a brief moment his hand was warm against hers, distracting her from reading the headline. Then she saw it. 'Destroy Dawn. Don't Let This Alien Take Over Our Planet.' She looked up from the flyer, planning to return it to him. He'd already moved along the line. She held the piece of paper out to Selene. "It's rubbish."

Selene chuckled. "You're the one that collects headlines." She pushed Piper's hand away.

"As if I want this one." She folded the piece of paper and looked around for somewhere to dispose of it. Not seeing anywhere, she leaned back so she could slide it into a pocket of her jeans, planning to get rid of it later.

Another argument, well behind her, had her trying to see what was happening. An old man was speaking loudly, a finger pointed at the boy's face as he held out a flyer. The boy shrugged and with a half smile moved to the next person who shook their head. Piper watched him a few seconds longer before she turned to Selene. She wasn't about to let anyone ruin this moment. Not with how long she'd been waiting to see the actual plant. And not only see it, but to touch and hold it.

She talked to her friend, trying to regain her earlier excitement. It didn't take long and her gaze frequently darted around to capture everything. There was no way she was going to be able to sleep tonight. She didn't want to miss a second of this day. She pulled out her communication device and recorded some of what was going on.

Selene took out her device and recorded Piper who continued her own recording. "Say something. Something really important that we'll be able to look back on and remember for the rest of our lives."

Piper tried, but all she could think of was the many news headlines she'd read over and over again. "I don't know what to say."

"You must be able to think of something."

"Why don't you say something?" Piper faced her communication device towards Selene. "Why do I have to come up with the quote we're going to look back on in years to come?"

Selene grinned. "Because I wouldn't have a clue what to say. The only word in my brain is 'yes' being repeated a million times."

Piper chuckled. "I can only think of things that have already been said, like 'A New Dawn for Mankind'. And that's someone else's quote. Not ours." She glanced around at the numerous people, the line having grown several metres behind them. "It looks like we're not the only ones excited to see Dawn. With all these people taking Dawn home, Dawn will never end." For a moment she thought about the boy who wanted to get rid of Dawn. There was no way she'd let that happen. Nor would anyone in this line. Or the lines that were likely forming at the many shops selling Dawn tomorrow. Thousands were waiting to welcome Dawn to Earth and into their homes. Actually, probably hundreds of thousands wished they could have a seedling. And like her, not all of them would be lucky enough to take one home.

"That's it. That's our quote. An endless dawn."

Piper grinned, meeting Selene's gaze. "Yes. That's our quote." She couldn't imagine life being any more perfect than it was at this moment. A pity her recording couldn't capture the feeling that raced through her, causing goosebumps to rise on her arms. Was this how people had felt all those decades ago when they'd waited to see the first step taken on the moon? Life brimming with possibilities, a thrill racing through her and anticipation keeping her on the edge of the seat.

As the night wore on, Piper grew tired. Even the streetlights didn't keep her from wanting to close her eyes. The noise from the crowd had dropped off, apart from the occasional crying baby, and as they passed midnight there was barely a sound. In an effort to stay awake longer, she turned to Selene. "Come for a walk?"

Selene stretched. "Only if that walk takes us to a toilet."

Piper nodded and waited for Selene to shake Evelyn's shoulder and let her know what they were doing.

Evelyn blinked several times, yawning. "Stay together and don't be gone too long."

"Okay, Mum." Selene turned to Piper. "Come on."

They walked silently to the public toilets where there were three lines. One in front of the door to the women's toilets, one in front of the men's and one in front of the all genders' toilets. The line to the women's toilet crept forward and two stalls became free one after the other. When Piper came out of the stall, she looked around for Selene as she washed her hands. Not knowing if Selene was in the stall or had finished, she headed outside. She spotted Selene confronting the boy who'd been handing out flyers earlier. He only had a handful left.

She reached Selene's side. "You ready to go?"

Selene barely glanced at her. She gestured towards the boy, her hand centimetres from his face. "Can you believe him? As if harassing people while they're waiting in line isn't bad enough, now he's hassling them as they're going to the toilet."

Chapter Three

Piper eyed the boy. He didn't seem bothered by Selene's comments. He actually appeared amused. "Don't worry about it. Let's go." She tugged on Selene's arm.

Selene shook her off. "Some people have to try and ruin everything." Her hands went to her hips as she glared at the boy.

"I think you've got that back to front. You're the one who came barrelling over to me. I wasn't hassling anyone." His amusement remained.

Selene gestured towards the flyers in his hand. "I'm not an idiot. You're standing around here waiting to give them to people."

The boy chuckled, turning his gaze on Piper. "Does she always jump to conclusions like this?"

She was tempted to return his grin, but that would make Selene crankier. Nor was she going to answer his question. It took her a few seconds to think of what to say to encourage Selene to forget the argument. Telling Selene she needed sleep would have gone over as well as returning the boy's grin. "Your mum will be worried if we're gone too much longer."

A girl strode towards them, stopping at the boy's side with only a brief look at the two of them. She had the same hazel eyes and sandy brown hair as the boy. Her hair almost reached her shoulders. "Sorry I took so long, Gibson. There were a million people waiting to use the toilet. I can't believe how many idiots think that buying a Dawn is a good idea."

"Idiots!" Selene took a step towards the girl.

Piper tried not to sigh, but was only half successful. Although she doubted Selene would have heard the soft sound over her own words.

"You're a pair of idiots."

The girl turned to Gibson. "I told you this'd be a waste of time. They're not interested in knowing the truth. A few pieces of paper aren't going to stop anything. Not now Dawns are being sold worldwide. It's too late for everyone. Including us."

Gibson shrugged. "Maybe it won't help. But it might slow things down. It was worth a try. Have a bit of faith, Zoe." His gaze returned to Piper. "If enough people listen, it might make a difference." He held her gaze a moment longer before he walked away, Zoe at his side shaking her head as she continued to disagree with him.

Piper watched them go. How could they not be excited about Dawn? It was the biggest discovery in what seemed like forever. Nothing else had come close to it in decades.

"Can you believe that pair?" Selene demanded.

Piper shrugged, not wanting to get into an argument with Selene when she was tired. They never ended well. "Your mum is probably getting worried."

Selene continued to complain as they wandered back to their seats. Piper tuned her out as she thought of the piece of paper in her pocket and the unsettling words Gibson and Zoe had spoken. What were they trying to slow down? The spread of Dawn? That was a good thing. There'd be no more pollution when enough people owned a plant. Dawn was exactly what their planet needed.

Reaching their seats, she noticed Evelyn was asleep. Sitting down, she thought of the headline about the attack on the Dawn laboratory. Had the two of them been a part of it? The boy's amused expression came to mind. He didn't seem the kind of person to attack guards and trash a building, causing millions of dollars worth of damage and months of setbacks in studying Dawn. But she didn't know him. For all she knew he could have been one of the masked people recorded by the security cameras. None of them had been caught so who knew what they looked like.

She drifted in and out of sleep, the blanket wrapped around her as she tried to get comfortable in the chair. She was excited and couldn't wait until the shop opened, but decided she should sleep. Particularly since she really wanted to enjoy the actual moment Selene bought Dawn. Being tired and cranky might take away from the experience. Although she was pretty sure nothing could do that. But why take the chance?

When the sun rose, parents tried to calm cranky children and hawkers walked up and down the line selling food and souvenirs. She checked the time. There were several hours before the shop, selling the seedlings, opened. The shopping complex had remained open all night as some of the larger shops had continued trading. After they'd eaten, they took turns heading to the toilets, which had longer lines than last night. As the time grew near, Piper kept checking her device, wishing time wouldn't go so slow. She drifted off to sleep, only to be woken by a noise from someone in the line. The moment she saw there was half an hour left, tiredness vanished and excitement raced through her. She couldn't stay still, yet she didn't dare move out of the line. Someone would take her place.

Piper and Selene waited in line while Evelyn returned everything to the vehicle, arriving back with five minutes to spare. The line crept forward and the air was motionless with an expectant silence. Even the babies were quiet. The line continued to move forward and Piper was finally able to see the shop through the open doors of the shopping complex. She had to stand on tiptoes and step slightly out of line, but it meant they were getting close.

The line moved several metres and her heart leapt as they stepped into the shopping complex and eventually reached the front door of the shop, stepping through it. They continued to move forward at a shuffle. Then she saw it, her first glimpse of Dawn. A man walked towards her, grinning as he kept glancing at the plant in his hands. It was in a recycled cardboard pot, some marketing gimmick used to promote Dawn's benefits to pollution. The plant was small, less than ten centimetres tall, and had two vivid green leaves. It looked ordinary. Piper knew from the numerous pictures she'd seen online that the seedling always looked ordinary. It wasn't until Dawn grew that she started to take on her characteristic looks. Vivid green leaves that were tear shaped, a vine like structure that was self-supporting and bell shaped flowers that wouldn't grow on these ones that had been genetically modified to prevent them from becoming a weed.

She spied another one, a woman walking behind the man, two children clutching her arms, their gazes fixed on the plant.

Selene gripped Piper's arm. "Aren't they beautiful?" Her voice was a reverent whisper.

Piper could only nod as she continued to shuffle forward with the rest of the crowd. Her heart leapt once again as she spied the trestle tables set up to deal with the flood of customers. Behind the tables were rows and rows of Dawns, sitting in their little cardboard pots on three timber tables. There was a large empty space on one of the tables, more than three quarters of it. If this was all the stock they had, not everyone in the line was going to be able to buy a plant. She wanted to be well away from here before people realised this.

As they reached the table Selene's hand tightened on Piper's arm before she let go. A woman held up a plant, not letting Selene take it until Evelyn had paid the woman standing beside her and filled in what they referred to as 'adoption papers'. From what Piper could see it was a fancy name for electronically collecting a person's details like name and address. She noticed Evelyn gave her work address, like she always gave to marketers.

Selene carefully took the plant, cradling the pot in both hands, her gaze focused on the seedling. "It's beautiful." Her words were a whisper.

The woman who'd handed over the plant held out a small bag. "Plant food. Make sure you follow the instructions."

Piper took the bag, wishing it was a plant. Her gaze was drawn back to Dawn.

Evelyn guided Selene away from the table. "Watch where you're walking. I didn't pay all that money for you to run into something and drop it before we get it out of the shop."

"Isn't it perfect?" Selene asked.

Piper nodded, taking Selene's arm to guide her so she didn't run into something like her mother predicted. "Absolutely." She wanted one of her own even more. Jealousy flared and she pushed it away. Nothing was going to ruin this moment. For a second she thought of Gibson. He had no idea what he was missing out on. Dawn was perfect. She dragged her gaze from the plant, scanning the area ahead of them. Nothing was in Selene's path.

The trip back to Selene's place was silent. Neither of them could take their gaze off Dawn once they were seated in the vehicle. Piper wanted to ask if she could hold the plant, but managed to remain silent. The bag of plant food was on the seat beside her. She started to reach for it so she could read the instructions, but stopped. There was no point. She doubted she'd be able to bring herself to look at anything other than Dawn. It was amazing. That little plant had come from a distant planet. The first alien brought to their world. She was desperate to hold it. Her hands curled into fists as she struggled to prevent herself from grabbing the plant. It wasn't hers. But she wished it was.

When they reached Selene's bedroom, the two of them sat on the bed staring at the seedling Selene held. The plant food was on the bedside drawers, neither of them interested in it when they had the plant to look at.

Selene yawned. "I am so unbelievably tired yet also wide awake. I doubt I'll be able to sleep."

"I know exactly what you mean." She reached for her communication device. "Can I take some pictures?"

"Sure. As long as you send a copy of them to me." Selene held out the plant.

Piper took several photos of both Selene and the plant then she moved her communication device closer rather than zooming in. When Dawn moved towards it, she grinned. "It looks like she's posing."

"How cool is that? If anyone ever said to me a few years ago that I'd be interested in plants, I'd have thought they were crazy. But Dawn is better than any old plant."

Piper took several more photos before she recorded Dawn following her communication device as she moved closely around it. When Selene put the plant on the bedside drawers Piper wanted to protest that she wasn't finished recording.

Selene stretched, yawning. "I'm so tired I might drop her."

Piper was tempted to say she could hold Dawn for a while, but didn't think it was time yet. Selene hadn't owned the plant a day. Maybe tomorrow she could ask to hold Dawn. She lay back against the bed, staring at the white ceiling. "I feel like my eyes are full of sand and I really need sleep, but my mind is ages away from shutting down."

Selene lay beside her. "When Dawn is big enough, we'll have to see if we can take cuttings and grow one for you. I know they said the plant would only grow from spores, but that doesn't mean a cutting won't work. Especially since they've made it so the seedlings they're selling won't produce spores. That's so unfair."

"Going by the statistics of the Dawns grown in the lab, that'll probably be about six months away." It seemed like an awfully long time to wait. Even further away than her birthday. It was a good thing Selene had one she could help take care of in the meantime.

"I wish you could have bought one."

Her eyelids felt heavy so she closed them for a moment. "Me too." Her words were slurred and she relaxed further, the bed extremely comfortable after the chair she'd spent the night in. Her thoughts became hazy, images of Dawn filling her mind.

Chapter Four

Rolling over, Piper was jarred awake when she bumped into Selene. At some stage she'd obviously drifted off to sleep. Stretching, she opened her eyes. Her first sight was of Dawn sitting on the drawers past Selene. She smiled. That was a view she could get used to every day. It was a pity she'd have to wait so long before they could try to propagate the plant. Her eyes narrowed and she sat up to have a closer look at Dawn.

"Did you have to wake me? I was having a really good dream." Selene rolled over, burying her face in the pillow.

"I think she's grown."

"What?" Selene turned to squint up at Piper.

"Dawn." She gestured towards the plant. "I think she's actually grown. Not much, maybe half a centimetre, but I'm sure she's grown. It might be as much as a centimetre."

Selene sat up to peer at the plant. "Impossible. They don't grow that quick."

"Let's measure her. That way we can keep track of how fast she grows."

"Sure. That sounds like a good idea." Selene stumbled out of bed.

It took them several minutes to decide where to keep track of Dawn. They sat the plant on the window ledge and made a mark on the side of the frame. Since it was where Selene planned to keep Dawn it seemed like a logical place to use for tracking the growth. That task done, the two of them decided to grab something to eat, both of them starving after their lengthy sleep.

Evelyn was in the kitchen. "I was wondering when you pair were going to wake up. You should check the news. They ran out of plants and ended up having to call the riot squad. People have been stealing them and there were a few people killed because they refused to give up their plants."

"Be right back." Selene ran from the room.

"What's wrong?" Evelyn looked from the doorway to Piper.

"We left Dawn on the window ledge."

Evelyn started to leave the room at the same time as Selene returned, cradling the plant. She pointed a finger at her daughter. "Don't tell anyone we bought that plant. The last thing we need is someone trying to break in and steal it." Evelyn slowly shook her head. "If I'd known how crazy people would behave I wouldn't have bought you one."

"I'm not stupid." Selene put the plant in the middle of the table. "Do you think she'll be all right here? Don't plants need light? Something other than these types of lights." She gestured upwards.

Piper stared at Dawn. It really wasn't fair. Selene knew next to nothing about looking after the plant. "They grew them under UV lamps in the lab. I'm sure you could do the same here. We can also see what else the lab website says about keeping Dawn inside." Maybe there'd be some new data. The website was usually updated every day or two. She'd visited it often enough to know how frequently it was updated.

Evelyn shook her head. "No you can't. Your parents called earlier and said you need to go home the moment you wake."

Piper wanted to protest. But she supposed they'd let her stay out longer than she'd expected. "I'll see what I can find out and message you later." She came forward, running a finger lightly over a leaf. "I can't wait until she's big enough we can try propagating her." The leaf tried to curl around her finger and she reluctantly pulled her hand away. It was almost like Dawn was sad to see her go. She pushed that fanciful idea aside. As amazing as Dawn was, she was only a plant.

When Piper reached home, she brought an abrupt end to her parent's questions by telling them she needed a shower. Resentment rushed through her. If they'd let her buy a plant they wouldn't have needed to ask their questions. They would have known first hand. It took all her willpower not to make that comment. She didn't want to be grounded and miss out on visiting Selene's Dawn every day.

Grabbing clothes from her bedroom, Piper started to head to the bathroom. She stopped at her door, remembering the flyer she'd shoved in her pocket. She drew it out and unfolded it, staring at the information, a website at the bottom. Out of curiosity she had a look on her device. An hour later she was still reading over the information, slowly shaking her head as she read the allegations.

The scientist, Kyndall, who'd created the website claimed he'd been one of the scientists who'd done the early testing on Dawn. He talked about the cutting he'd smuggled out of the lab to prove the genetic modifications they'd made hadn't worked. The plant had shown signs of minute alterations to the changed DNA. He'd believed it was the plant and not human error that had caused the anomalies. According to Kyndall, Dawn was able to return to original form no matter what changes they made. Given enough time, the plant was capable of overriding the changes. Looking at the results of Kyndall's experiments it didn't look like a great deal of time was needed. It depended on how quickly the plant grew.

Piper didn't believe a word she read. How could it be possible? There was no way the Dawn Project would have sold plants if they were as harmful as Kyndall claimed. And if the spores did get in your lungs and grow, causing things like coughing up blood and eventually death, the plants being sold couldn't produce spores. Not that she believed him. There hadn't been a single comment in all the reports on Dawn that proved his allegations. Someone would have said something. They were pretty significant problems. It would have been impossible to hide them from the world.

It was lies. Whoever was running this website couldn't be one of the early scientists who'd experimented on Dawn. None of them would have tried to ruin such a momentous moment in history. And she wasn't about to let him ruin it for her. Dawn was the most amazing thing to have happened in her life. Absolutely no one was going to ruin that for her. Not her parents, not Gibson and certainly not some fake scientist.

She did a search on Kyndall's name, finding news articles. One of them talked about how he'd accepted money from competitors to undermine what was being done with Dawn. The final article she read was about his suicide and his children, Gibson and Zoe. She stared at the images, feeling sympathy that they couldn't accept the truth about their father and had resorted to handing out flyers. She closed down the webpages she'd opened and brought up an image of Dawn. One day soon she'd have a plant. She wouldn't stop saving in case they weren't able to grow one from a cutting. Maybe by the time they released the second lot of stock she'd have enough money for one.

Setting aside her communication device, she headed to the bathroom. After she'd finished in there she did what she should have done earlier and went on the real website. The one that talked about how best to care for Dawn. Several hours later she sent Selene a message containing the relevant information about raising Dawn indoors before she joined her parents for dinner.

During the meal she answered their many questions about being with Selene when she bought Dawn. She told them almost everything. She didn't mention Gibson and his flyers. It was bad enough that they'd seen the news stories about the riots and thefts. They didn't need more information that would keep them from letting her buy a plant. She was sure that things would settle down and everyone who wanted a Dawn would be able to buy one during the next release.

When the meal was over, Piper headed to her room, pushing aside thoughts of Gibson. She knew why she hadn't wanted her parents to know about him, but couldn't decide why she didn't want to think about him. Her dad often said there was no smoke without fire. But sometimes the only smoke was that which was created by different problems. Ones not remotely related. That didn't help her figure out why she didn't want to think about Gibson. She tried to tell herself it was because she didn't want him or his sister to tarnish the occasion. But that didn't seem right.

Closing her bedroom door, she sat at her desk and wrote about Dawn in her journal. She tried to capture every second of her first encounter, even writing about Gibson. What would it have been like to have a father willing to do that? She couldn't imagine her dad doing anything similar to what Kyndall had done. How could someone she knew and loved think of being so dishonest? Was that it? Was that why they couldn't believe he'd been wrong? She didn't have a clue and there was no point in making up reasons. She didn't know anything about Gibson's family, other than what she'd read online. Gibson's amused expression came to mind. She pushed it away. She didn't know him and had no interest in knowing him or his sister. But she couldn't get him out of her mind. Maybe that was it. She felt sorry for him that his father had ruined Dawn for him. That he could never be a part of such a momentous occasion.

In the end, she sent him a message using the contact details on the website. *Gibson, I'm sorry about your father. Piper.*

A reply came through a moment later. *I don't need sympathy. I need people to believe Dawn is dangerous. She'll destroy our planet. Gib.*

She stared at the words, slowly shaking her head. He was wrong, but obviously nothing she said would make a difference. Gibson would always believe his father and the man was no longer alive to take back his lies. She deleted the message, putting her communication device on her bedside cabinet. He'd end up like his father. Sorrow washed over her. He didn't need sympathy. What he needed was her pity.

That night she dreamt about propagating Dawn and bringing her own plant home, waking the next morning with a smile. The first thing she did, before getting out of bed, was send Selene a message asking about Dawn. The reply came back immediately.

Growing!!!

She doubted it. Selene had a tendency to exaggerate. *Be over as soon as I've had breakfast.*

Piper was ready in record time. Rushing out the front door, grudgingly promising her parents she wouldn't be next door all day. While she waited for the elevator, a message came through. Expecting it to be from Selene, asking where she was, she checked it.

Piper, sorry about last night. I should have checked first before assuming you were one of the people who bought a Dawn. Gib.

She almost didn't answer, but decided that would be rude. *Gib, I am one of the people who wanted to buy Dawn and waited in line all night to catch my first glimpse. I couldn't buy a plant this time, but I'm hoping I can next time. Piper.*

A reply came back almost instantly. *Then you're one of the lucky ones.*

Sorrow washed over her, along with anger at his father. *How can you say that? Dawn is the discovery of a lifetime. You shouldn't believe everything you're told, no matter who it is that tells you.*

She entered the elevator as the next reply arrived. *I believe what I've seen with my own eyes. Maybe you should think about your own advice.*

Glaring at the screen, she stepped out of the elevator and into the foyer, refusing to answer, all sympathy vanishing. Independent scientists had been brought in to examine Dawn. They'd been full of praise for the plant and what she could do for the future of their planet. Maybe the early samples, before they'd been modified, hadn't been safe. But things had changed. His father hadn't been with the Dawn Project long enough to learn that. He'd sold out instead.

Another message arrived as she entered Selene's building. *Which of the ones from Friday night were you?*

She waited by the elevator, trying to decide if she should reply. *The one with the friend who accused you of handing out flyers to people lining up at the toilets.*

The one with the warm hands.

She stared at the screen, stumbling as she entered

the elevator. That was what he'd remembered about her? His hands had been equally as warm. She tried to think how to reply. What did one say to that? Every comment she came up with seemed lame. *Better than cold hands.*

So it is.

Reaching Selene's floor, she decided not to reply. Not that she knew what she could say. It was probably best not to talk to him. As intriguing as she found him, there was no way they could ever agree about Dawn.

When she reached Selene's room, where Dawn sat on the bedside drawers, she stared at the plant. "What did you do to her?"

"Nothing."

"You must have. She's doubled in size. She shouldn't have grown this fast. None of the lab tests showed results like this." Some of the results she'd read on Kyndall's website came to mind and she firmly pushed them aside. None of that information was real. Everyone else told a different story. Gibson and his family had no idea.

Selene shook her head. "She was like this when I woke up. Here, look at this." She showed Piper a photo on her communication device.

Chapter Five

Piper stared at the communication device. The image showed Dawn sitting beside the lamp on the bedside drawers. The plastic lampshade had disappeared and Dawn was wrapped around the metal frame where the shade had once been, as if the frame was a trellis. One tendril was inside the bag of plant food that had been left beside the lamp. "Where's the lampshade?"

Selene shrugged. "I don't know. I think she might have eaten it."

Piper grinned. Obviously Selene was joking. "Okay. Sure." She pointed at the plant food in the picture. "This is probably the cause of her growth. They said a teaspoon a day, not let her have as much as she wants."

"She ate half the bag."

"You do know plants don't eat. Well, not like people and animals do."

"Maybe not ordinary plants, but Dawn is different."

Piper eyed Selene's expression. Her glare and stubborn look guaranteed that no matter what Piper said, Selene was going to argue it. That was the last thing she wanted to do. That would lead to a fight and Selene kicking her out, calling her later to apologise and say what a terrible friend she was. It would also mean she'd miss out on seeing Dawn. "Have you measured her yet?"

Selene shook her head.

"Are we going to use the window frame?" She didn't want anyone to steal the plant, but surely a few seconds on the ledge wouldn't hurt.

"I guess." Selene sat the plant on the window ledge while Piper used the pencil left on the ledge to mark Dawn's height.

Piper stared at the two marks while Selene returned Dawn to the bedside drawers. It didn't seem possible. "Maybe you shouldn't give Dawn any plant food for a few days."

"That's what I was thinking." Selene joined her by the window, sliding it open further.

Piper stared at the busy road below. "I can't stay long. My parents said I can't be here all day."

"Aww. I wanted you to come with me to buy a light bulb."

There was no way her parents would agree to that. "We can go tomorrow after school. Dawn should be okay for another day." She grinned. "It doesn't seem to have bothered her so far. Not with how much she's grown."

"I guess. But I really wanted to go today."

Piper turned away from the window. "Mind if I take some more photos?"

Selene laughed. "I'm surprised you didn't want to take them the moment you arrived."

Piper grinned, not bothering to say that she had. Taking out her communication device, she noticed an unread message. Ignoring it, she took the photos. Selene would want to know who it was from if she read it now and if it was Gibson, there was no way she could explain how she'd ended up in a conversation with him.

It wasn't until nearly bedtime that Piper remembered her unread message. Like she'd assumed, it was from Gibson. She stared at the words, not sure how to reply. *Can I show you what Dawn does so you can see for yourself? See with your own eyes that what I said is true.*

You're a stranger. I'm not crazy. Which I'd have to be to go somewhere with a complete stranger.

Meet me somewhere public and get to know me.

She was tempted to say yes. Taking a deep breath, she reminded herself to be practical. To tell him no. But she couldn't bring herself to send the message she knew she should send. *I'll think about it.*

Okay. You can choose the location.

Setting her communication device on her bedside cabinet, she returned to the living room to say goodnight to her parents.

Alistair gestured towards the news they were watching. "Should have bought you a plant. People are offering ten thousand if those who managed to buy one will sell to them."

"As if I'd sell Dawn," Piper said.

"Then we should have bought one for ourselves as an investment," Alistair said.

Tricia slowly shook her head. "I never would have expected people to pay such ridiculous prices."

Piper guessed it was best to keep to herself that she would have paid any price to have a plant. Including ten thousand even if that was all the money she had. "I'm heading to bed. Night." She came forward to kiss each of her parents.

Tricia captured her hand and drew her back when

she would have returned to her room. "I know how much the plant means to you, but with all the craziness going on about it, you're probably lucky you didn't get one. We'll buy one for you when everything settles down and it isn't such a rarity."

It took a ridiculous amount of willpower to smile. "Thanks." She managed not to say it'd be too late by then. She'd lost the chance to be a part of Dawn's beginning. A major part, not a minor one.

The next morning, Piper rushed to get ready for school so she could visit Selene and see Dawn first. Would the plant have grown or had yesterday's growth spurt been from the excessive amount of plant food? She couldn't wait to find out.

Selene waited for her at the door to the apartment. "You should see Dawn now." Selene grabbed her arm, tugging her towards the bedroom.

Piper eyed the plant, now in a large ceramic pot. She had to have grown at least five centimetres since yesterday. "You haven't given her more plant food, have you?"

"She got into it again. I've put it away now."

"She's only meant to have a teaspoon a day."

"I know. You don't have to keep telling me. It wasn't like I deliberately gave it to her."

Piper started to point out that Selene should have

known after yesterday, but managed to keep the comment to herself. It wasn't fair. She wouldn't have left the food lying around. If Selene wasn't careful, she was going to kill the plant. "What are you going to do with Dawn while we're at school?"

"Leave her in my room. I'll close the windows and leave the light on. I didn't get a chance to buy one of those light bulbs yesterday. I forgot when I bought the ceramic pot. Do you know how hard it is to find unglazed and unpainted ceramic pots? I didn't realise how difficult not being able to use plastic containers was going to be."

Piper glanced around the room. "We can pick up a light bulb for Dawn this afternoon after school."

"Cool." Selene grabbed her schoolbag and headed for the bedroom door, pausing to look at Dawn. "Do you think she'll be okay?"

Piper stared at the plant, hoping the extra plant food didn't kill Dawn. But Selene wasn't looking for facts. She wanted to be reassured. "Yeah. Dawn will be fine." Somehow she'd make sure of it. She followed Selene out of the room, unable to resist having a last look over her shoulder. Why couldn't she have been the one who'd been able to buy a plant?

The day seemed to be unbearably long and Piper nearly ran from her final class, meeting up with

Selene to walk with her to a nearby shopping complex. They strode through the complex to a lighting shop, surprised by how few UV bulbs were left on the shelves.

Piper held one out to Selene. "Lucky you didn't leave it much longer or they would have sold out." Had everyone who'd bought a plant decided to keep it hidden away? Not that she blamed them. She wouldn't want to risk losing Dawn either.

Selene took the boxed light bulb. "I guess everyone is worried."

A man came closer, nodding towards the light bulb. "You one of the lucky ones to get a Dawn?"

There was something about him that made Piper want to run. It wasn't the way he looked. That was ordinary enough with his medium brown hair, blue eyes and a light tan. Or the way he held himself or the casual clothes he wore. She couldn't work it out, but everything screamed 'run'. She stepped in front of Selene, ready to run if necessary. "I wish. We're amongst the unlucky ones." She tried to smile, but it felt forced.

"Then what's with the bulb?"

"Ferns." Piper blurted out the word. "I think it's the wrong option, but my friend disagrees and they're her ferns. She heard how the UV bulbs work for

Dawn so thought they'd work for her ferns since they're dying."

Selene stepped around Piper to stand beside her. She grinned. "And I'm always right, so we'll buy the bulb." She glanced at Piper, a question in her eyes.

Piper wished she could tell her how she felt, but that would have given them away. "Not always. Do you need me to list how many times you've been wrong?"

Selene chuckled. "That wouldn't take long. The incidents are almost non existent." She looked at the man. "But like my friend said, the information about Dawn made me think the UV light would work for my ferns. It shouldn't be as harsh as sunlight and they do need some light. My home is super dark. Not enough windows. I'm sick of them dying so decided to try this bulb."

"Excuse me." A woman reached past them for a light bulb.

There was a moment of awkward silence as the woman walked away. The man nodded to the light bulb Selene held. "Good luck with your ferns." He followed the woman towards the check out.

Piper watched him strike up a conversation with the vaguely familiar woman, too far from them to hear what was said.

Selene leaned close before she spoke. "He gives me the creeps. What made you lie to him?"

"He gives me the creeps too."

They waited until the man had left the shop before they paid for the light bulb and headed home. The entire walk Piper kept glancing over her shoulder, feeling like someone watched her. Each time she checked, there was no one there. Obviously the man had bothered her more than she'd realised.

Chapter Six

The next three days Piper was at Selene's every chance she had. Her parents complained they hardly saw her and she couldn't expect to spend so much time there each day. It took some effort, but Piper eventually convinced them the novelty would wear off and she wouldn't be at Selene's so much. Although she was pretty certain the novelty wasn't about to wear off anytime soon and her parents probably knew that. But for now, they let her keep visiting Selene morning and afternoon. A couple of times she thought about messaging Gibson and telling him she'd decided not to meet him. She'd gotten as far as starting the message before deleting it. Telling him no was the sensible option. Why couldn't she convince herself? His amused expression came to mind followed by an image of him she'd seen online.

Looking sad, his arm around his sister as if to protect her from the journalists.

Friday after school, Piper stared at Dawn. The plant had to be half a metre tall and there were another three leaves that had unfurled while they'd been at school, four more looking like they were forming. She took a second look at one of the buds. It seemed different to the other ones. It was an almost translucent green. Had it somehow been damaged? Or maybe Dawn was lacking nutrients. Which wouldn't surprise her with how quickly the plant had grown. It might be time for Selene to start giving the plant food again. She reached out a finger to touch the bud, but stopped, worried she might damage it further.

Selene came into the bedroom with two bottles of water. She handed one to Piper before opening her own. "She's growing fast, isn't she?"

Piper nodded, swallowing a mouthful of water. "A lot faster than she should be. Are you sure you're not doing anything to cause it?"

"Maybe I should be the one asking you that question. You do more with her than I do."

"I'm only following the scientists' recommendations." Other than giving her plant food every day. "Maybe I should read the information again. I mean, it's great that she's growing fast, but maybe she's growing too fast. Even humans have problems when they grow fast."

"It could be that our environment is more polluted than we thought. She's meant to thrive on pollution."

Piper stared at the vivid green plant, her gaze drawn to the bud. It reminded her of something, but she couldn't think what. Then it hit her. A flower. It reminded her of the few images she'd seen of flowers forming on Dawn. The scientists had made the plants sterile so they couldn't breed. Surely she had to be wrong.

"She can't be that fascinating that you want to stand and stare at her all afternoon. You never want to do anything these days except tend Dawn."

It hadn't taken her long to realise that owning Dawn was wasted on Selene. She was already growing bored with looking after the plant. "I was thinking. Anyway, I should head home. My parents have been complaining about how much time I've been spending over here." She wanted to look at some of the images, she'd saved in her journal, without Selene asking her what she was doing. If she was wrong, she didn't want Selene teasing her about it for weeks.

Selene giggled. "Yeah, my mum asked if you were planning to move in."

She shared a look with Selene, grinning. "Didn't we try that in primary school?"

"I'd almost forgotten about that. It took me ages to put my stuff back in my room. I don't know why we didn't pick my room to move into since it's bigger."

Piper shrugged, not wanting to remind Selene it was because she'd not only wanted a sister, but also a father. "I better go before they start saying I can't come over at all."

Selene walked her to the elevator, waving her off as she entered. Piper couldn't stop thinking about the bud that had looked different. She had to be wrong. The scientists had modified Dawn so she didn't risk becoming a pest. They'd cited reasons such as the cane toads that had been introduced generations ago and were still a problem in Australia. There was no way they'd have released Dawn to the public if she posed a threat to the environment.

Stepping out of the elevator, she stepped straight back in. "Close door." The door shut, cutting off her view of the man who'd talked to them when they'd bought the light bulb Monday after school. What was he doing here?

The elevator began to move and she looked at the

lit up numbers. Someone else obviously wanted to use it. When the elevator stopped on the second floor, she stepped out, returning the nod an elderly man gave her in greeting. Turning, she faced the closed doors of the elevator. What was she going to do?

Calling Selene, she wandered towards the stairs.

Selene answered immediately. "She's fine." There was humour in her voice. "I haven't killed her off and before you ask, no I'm not going to send you any photos."

"That man is downstairs." She kept her voice low.

"What man?" The humour vanished from Selene's voice.

"The one who gave us both the creeps." She started down the stairs, her voice sounding odd in the stairwell.

"Maybe he knows someone here."

Piper could hear it in Selene's voice that she didn't believe her words. "Maybe."

"Did he see you?"

"No. I went back into the elevator before he could. He was looking outside. Like he was waiting for something." Or someone. She reached the first floor, hesitating before she continued down the next flight to the ground floor.

"Do you want me to come downstairs?"

She didn't reply immediately. "No. It's okay. I'll see if he's still there."

"If he is, come back to my place. Don't go anywhere near him. You can stay here until he goes. Even stay the night if you want."

She couldn't go back to Selene's place. Not without telling her parents why she wasn't coming home and that would lead to them not letting her visit Selene on her own ever again. "I'm having a look now." She opened the door to peer into the foyer. The man was there. Her stomach lurched. What was she going to do?

"Well? Can you see him?"

Before she could answer Selene, or come up with a plan, the woman who'd bought a UV light the same time they had, entered the building. She smiled in greeting at the man, coming forward to clasp his hand.

"Piper? Are you okay?" There was fear in Selene's voice.

"Sorry. He knows someone here." She hesitated. Had he known the woman before she'd bought the light bulb?

"That's okay then." Selene laughed, a nervous sound. "Guess we were worried for no reason."

"Yeah. I suppose so." Piper hesitated. Should she

tell Selene who the man knew? It could have been a coincidence. She didn't want to worry Selene when she didn't know for certain. "I'll see you tomorrow morning before school." Waiting until the man and woman were in the elevator, she stepped into the foyer.

"Only because you want to visit Dawn. I never saw you anywhere near this much before I bought her."

Piper headed outside, glancing around the area. Everything seemed normal. No strange men lurking about. "You make it sound like I never visited. I probably spent half my time at your place."

"Yeah, but these days we don't spend any time at your place."

She couldn't exactly argue that comment. Reaching her apartment building, she stepped inside. "I better go. I'm nearly home."

"See you in the morning."

She smiled at the teasing note in her friend's voice, saying goodbye before she disconnected the call.

Chapter Seven

When Piper arrived home, she barely paused to say hello to her parents, who both worked from home, before heading to her room. She needed to figure out what the bud was. At her desk she first checked the images she'd saved before she looked online for more images of Dawn. The ones she had weren't good enough to help her figure it out. She tried not to think of the website that Gibson's flyer had directed her to. There was no way the Dawn project would have sold the plants if there was anything wrong with them.

Relief hit her when she read the words in one of the articles she found. Flowers were not uncommon. They were sterile and couldn't produce spores, but they did take nutrients away from the plant and people should remove them and double the amount of plant food they were giving their plant. Leaving them grow would risk weakening the plant. She smiled wryly, glad she could stop worrying. Kyndall's website had obviously been full of lies. She should try and forget about it instead of thinking of the horror stories she'd found on it. Why couldn't Gibson accept that his father had lied to everyone and take the website down?

Out of curiosity, she decided to see if they'd retracted any of the lies Kyndall had told or if they'd shut down the website. When a page appeared telling her the website didn't exist, she typed the address in once more, being extra careful to get it correct. It didn't help. She had the same result. Relief hit her. They'd stopped trying to spread their father's lies. Exiting the page, she sent a message to Gibson. *When did you take down the website?*

A few seconds later she received a message to say the number was no longer in service. She stared at her communication device. What was going on? Both the website and Gibson's number were no longer in use? Goosebumps rose on her arms and she rubbed them. An unpleasant feeling accompanied the goosebumps.

A message came through. Not recognising who it was from, it took her a moment to decide if she should read it.

Piper, I thought you weren't going to get back to me. When they shut down the website and started monitoring our devices I thought you wouldn't want my new number. Gib.

How did you know I tried to contact you?

We've been monitoring those trying to access the old website and our old numbers. I don't know how long you'll be able to reach me at this number, but in future I'll message you if I have to change numbers.

Piper stared at the message, reading it several times. After seeing the strange man at Selene's apartment building, Gibson's words were more unsettling than they should be. *Who shut down the website?*

The authorities. When you have the kind of money the Dawn Project now has you can afford to pay the corrupt to do your work for you.

She sighed. He was obviously getting worse. His amused expression came to mind. It was a pity. From the few minutes she'd spent with him, she'd had the feeling she might have found him interesting. If he hadn't let his father's crazy ideas infect him.

Deciding it was best not to contact him again, she closed the message. He was a lot crazier than she'd first thought. She sent a message to Selene. *The pale green bud that's forming is a flower. They're typical and nothing to worry about, but you need to remove it and give Dawn two teaspoons of plant food a day so it doesn't make her sick.*

Why didn't you say something earlier?

I wanted to make certain first.

Mum is going to be annoyed. She was livid about how much Dawn has already eaten. She said for the price we paid, they should have included a larger bag.

It's important to double the food. You don't want her to die.

When her communication device remained silent, she started her homework, putting it aside well before it was finished. There was too much going on for her to focus properly. She decided to join her parents in the living room where they were probably watching the news. Spending time with them might stop some of their complaints about how often she was at Selene's place. She doubted it, but it was worth a try.

She almost fell asleep watching the news, an image of Selene's apartment building waking her fully. "What's going on?"

"Shh." Tricia made a shushing motion with her hand.

An image of the woman who'd bought the light bulb was projected onto the wall. "Found this evening by her visiting daughter, Ms Weets is the latest victim of a home invasion related to Dawn." The image was replaced by that of an advanced plant. "Ms Weets' daughter fears her mother will never regain consciousness to give details of her attacker."

Alistair gestured towards the images as the reporter listed some of the many home invasions that had occurred since the release of Dawn. "This is what happens when everyone is convinced they need something and there's not enough to go around. What did they expect with all the hype?"

Piper couldn't help thinking about the strange man. Surely he wasn't the one who'd attacked Ms Weets. It had to be a coincidence. She wasn't about to let Gibson's crazy theories infect her. Rising to her feet, she interrupted her parents' discussion. "I should probably finish my homework." As she walked to her room, she heard them return to their discussion about Dawn. There was no way they were going to let her buy one. Not with the comments they were making. Her heart sank. The only way she'd get one any time soon was if they could propagate Selene's plant and even then her parents wouldn't be keen for her to have it.

After the attack on Ms Weets, Piper's parents wouldn't let her visit Selene on the weekend. She tried to convince them that the criminal already had what they wanted and there was no reason for them to return, but it didn't help. It got worse when Ms Weets died Saturday night. They worried someone would learn Selene had a plant. Piper told them over and over again that they'd kept it a secret, not even telling the kids at school. It wasn't until Monday, after school, that she was able to see Dawn again. Her parents didn't know she was visiting so she couldn't stay for long without having them wonder where she was.

She stared at the plant, which was now in a larger ceramic pot. She wished she'd been there on the weekend when Selene had potted Dawn. This was the second time she'd missed out on helping put the plant in a new pot. "I thought you said you removed the flower." The plant had to be a metre tall.

"I did, but another grew back."

"So remove it."

"I really want to find out what one looks like. I've been wondering ever since I removed the first one. They look so pretty in the pictures."

"What if it makes the plant sick? Have you been giving her extra plant food? Do you want to risk losing Dawn?"

Selene shook her head. "Of course I don't want her to die, but she looks fine. The moment she stops looking fine I'll remove the flower. And I can't give her extra plant food. I accidentally left it out Saturday night and she ate it. All of it. Mum said she's not buying me any until next month. That I should have been more careful."

Piper checked over the plant. She looked healthy. Selene was right, there was nothing wrong with Dawn. "Okay. Make sure you watch her carefully."

"Whose plant is it?"

"Fine. But you know you'd be annoyed if you let her die." She thought it best to drop the topic before she was the one who annoyed Selene. It wasn't like she could argue the comment. It was Selene's plant. But Piper couldn't help wishing she could remove the flower. Why risk losing such a valuable plant? It didn't make sense. After a few more minutes, she told Selene she had to go.

"It isn't fair. Your parents are being ridiculous. No one knows I have a plant. It's driving me crazy not being able to tell anyone. When will they let you visit again?"

Piper shrugged. "I'll keep asking. They'll eventually give in." She paused a moment. "I better go before they're looking for me."

Selene sighed heavily. "I'll see you at school tomorrow."

Chapter Eight

All week Piper had to keep reminding herself not to pester Selene about the flower. Each day after school she spent a few minutes at Selene's as she wasn't allowed to visit. It took all her willpower not to stay long. Each day she begged to visit Selene, pointing out that there'd been no more problems at the apartment building. No break ins and no attacks. They said on the news that Ms Weets had been the only woman in the building with a plant and the only resident who'd been attacked. It was that bit of information that finally convinced Piper's parents, Friday afternoon, that she could visit Selene again. She hadn't had the chance to visit today since she'd been late leaving school.

She tried not to be too enthusiastic. Jumping around the living room and victory punching the air probably wasn't the best idea. It'd only annoy her parents. "Thank you. You don't know how much this means to me."

"I think we have a bit of an idea," Alistair said dryly.

"Don't be over there all evening. An hour tops," Tricia said.

"Okay." She hurried from the apartment before they could change their mind. Reaching the elevator, it didn't take long for it to arrive and she stepped in, sending a message to Selene. *They finally said yes. I'll be there in a couple of minutes.*

When the elevator stopped twice to let people in she began to grow impatient. Didn't they realise they were holding her up? Okay, of course they didn't, but why did everyone need to go out now?

Piper reached the ground floor and stepped out of the elevator, checking the message that came through. As she expected, it was from Selene. *Don't come over, mum is sick and I think I might be getting sick too. I'll send you a picture of the flower in full bloom.*

An image came through and she looked at the bell like, white flower. She really wanted to see it for herself. This wasn't fair. Just when her parents had relented. *How sick? Can I come over for five minutes for a quick look?*

Maybe later. We're heading to the hospital. Mum's

finding it difficult to breathe. Like always. I'll call you when we get home.

Disappointment washed over her. *Okay. Hope it's nothing major.*

It never is. Just annoying.

Piper headed back to her place calling out as she stepped in the front door, "It's only me. I'm back."

"Is everything okay?" Tricia asked. "Your hour isn't up yet."

Piper nodded, then shrugged. "I guess. Selene's mum isn't well. They've gone to the hospital. She'll call me later to let me know when I can come over."

"Is she having problems with her breathing?" Alistair asked.

"Yeah."

Tricia shared a look with Alistair. "It always ends up on her lungs whenever she gets sick. A pity she can't afford to do something permanent about the problem. Her sister's the same."

"If they made healthcare more affordable it'd cost the government less in the long run," Alistair said.

Not wanting to get drawn into a conversation that would bore her, Piper backed away. "I should probably start my homework." She escaped to her room, her parents barely pausing in their discussion about what was wrong with the health system. She slumped into the chair at her desk. How long would it take for Evelyn to see a doctor? Would they be back early enough for her to visit? She tried to think how long they'd been gone the last time Evelyn had been sick. She was sure it had been less than two hours. Hopefully that was all the time it took before she could see Dawn. Even though she was worried about what the flower might be doing to the plant's health, she was excited about seeing it. The only people who'd seen Dawn in flower were the scientists on the Dawn Project.

Too excited about the prospect of seeing Dawn in bloom to do her homework, Piper did her usual search through the news reports about Dawn. There were no details about when the next lot would be available. After that she forced herself to concentrate on her homework, relieved to eventually finish it. Checking the time, she wondered how much longer Selene and Evelyn would be. Before she had the chance to contact Selene and ask, her mum called her to dinner. She hadn't heard from Selene by the time dinner was over. Looking for messages again, she found none, sending one of her own.

Is everything okay? She stared at the communication device, waiting for a reply. There was none. She hadn't heard back by the time she went to bed.

The first thing she did the next morning was check her messages. There were none from Selene so she sent another one. *What happened to my reply? Did you forget about me?*

No message came through. Was Evelyn that sick? Maybe there was something going around. She checked the latest news reports and found nothing. Not knowing what else to do, Piper had breakfast.

All day she kept checking for messages. Selene remained silent. The weekend dragged and she hadn't heard from Selene by Monday morning. The only person she heard from was Gibson, letting her know he had a new number. She almost answered him, reminding herself several times that he was crazy before she closed his message.

Selene wasn't at school Monday morning. Nor the following days. By Thursday, when Piper still hadn't heard from Selene, she told her mum.

"I was wondering why you'd stopped pestering me to visit. I thought the pair of you might be fighting. Do you want me to call the hospital?" Tricia asked.

"How would that help?" She was starting to wonder why she'd bothered saying anything. It looked like it had been a waste of time.

"Maybe Evelyn is really sick this time and had to stay there."

She hadn't thought of that. "Okay." Piper paced back and forth while she waited for her mum to finish talking to the hospital. It seemed to take forever. She smiled slightly when she heard her mum say she was Evelyn's sister, Linda.

Eventually, Tricia finished the call. "The hospital said their system shows they never turned up and suggests we try visiting them. Do you want me to come with you?"

Piper shook her head, feeling like an idiot that she hadn't thought of doing that herself. But Selene hadn't answered her numerous calls and messages so she'd assumed she wasn't home. "No, I'll be right."

She went to the apartment building next door and stood looking at the door for several minutes before she knocked on it. When there was no answer she went to the underground parking garage and found their bay empty. She stared at the space feeling sick. Where was Selene? Uneasiness rushed through her. Using her communication device she sent Selene another message.

Please answer me. I'm worried. Like all her recent messages, it remained unanswered. She couldn't help thinking about Gibson and his father's dire predictions. She pushed those concerns aside. They weren't true. What she should be worried about, other than Selene and Evelyn, was Dawn left unattended for days. How long could the plant survive without care? Maybe Gibson would know. It wasn't like there was anyone else she could ask. *Can I ask you a few questions about Dawn without you exaggerating?* No message came back. Maybe something was wrong with her communication device. Selene might have sent her a reply and she hadn't received it.

When a message came through a few seconds later, she half expected it to be Gibson. It wasn't. Her mum had sent a message. *Are they there?*

She stared at the communication device for a minute before she could bring herself to answer. Obviously it wasn't an issue with the device. *No. I'll be home shortly.*

Her mum met her at the front door. "I called Linda. She hasn't heard from them either. She's going to call some friends and see if she can find out what's going on."

Piper nodded, wishing there was something she could do. In her room, she checked Kyndall's website. She received an error code. Had Gibson given up expecting a reply from her? It had been a fortnight since she'd replied to any of his messages so she couldn't really blame him. She'd given up expecting a reply when one came.

What did you want to know?

Instead of sending a message, she called him, setting the device to voice only.

"Hello, Piper."

"Hi." She struggled to think how to ask him what she wanted to know. It wasn't her plant and he knew that. Who worried about an unattended plant when their friend was missing? She guessed she was worried about both.

"Is something wrong?"

She hesitated. "I'm not sure."

"There's only one way to find out." His voice was filled with humour.

All of a sudden she felt stupid. What little he knew about Dawn he'd learned from his father and she should be focused on trying to figure out where Selene was. Not worrying about Dawn too. "Actually, you probably can't help. Sorry I called." Speaking to Gibson made her think of Kyndall's lies. Nothing that had been on his website was true. Dawn couldn't make people sick or kill them.

"Wait up. How do you know I can't help?"

For all she knew, Selene and Evelyn were well and had taken off somewhere, Selene's message not going through. That happened sometimes. Messages didn't always go through. "Unless you can find missing people, I don't see how you can." She started to tell him goodbye.

"Is this something to do with Dawn? Were they sick before they disappeared? Did they let a flower grow?"

Chapter Nine

Words caught in Piper's throat. Gibson had described the situation perfectly. How had he known? She made her way unsteadily to her bed and sat heavily on it.

"You there, Piper?"

"Yes." The word was barely a whisper. "How did you know?"

"You're not the first call. We've had several calls and messages. All of them the same. People who've tried to contact us through the old website."

She pressed her fingers against her mouth to hold back the many protests she wanted to make. Surely he must be mistaken. He couldn't believe their disappearances were related to Dawn. She was tempted to hang up, but even though she expected him to say no or laugh, she asked, "Can you help me find Selene?" She'd ignored him for a fortnight.

Why would he say yes? And how would he know where Selene was? She was obviously more worried about her friend than she'd thought if she was asking desperate questions like that.

"Give me an address where I can meet you. I'll see what I can do."

Surprise kept her silent for a few seconds. "You can help?"

"I can't promise anything. But I'll see what I can do. Where do you live?"

She hesitated. He was a stranger, but she was desperate to find out what had happened to Selene. She kept telling herself there was no way he could know what had happened to her friend, but she couldn't take the chance that there was a possibility he did know. She rattled off Selene's address, unwilling to give her own.

"Okay, give me half an hour. We're actually not far from there at the moment. I'll meet you out the front."

She didn't have a chance to reply, or ask him what he meant by 'we', before he disconnected. She stared at the communication device. She was crazy. And desperate. It took her several minutes before she could bring herself to rise to her feet and walk to the living room, trying to act normal. Both her parents were sitting on the couch, quietly talking. Her gaze was momentarily drawn to the news that no one watched before she focused on her parents. "I'm going to try knocking on the door again. In case they were too sick to hear me earlier."

"Linda will be there in less than two hours," Tricia said.

They'd given her the perfect excuse not to come straight back home. "Okay. I might wait there for her if Selene doesn't let me in."

"Make sure you wait in the foyer. Don't hang around out the front," Alistair said.

She nodded before going next door. Arriving, she couldn't resist taking the lift to Selene's floor and knocking on the apartment door several more times. There was no answer. Giving up, she waited in the foyer, watching for Gibson. It was a little less than half an hour when a vehicle pulled up out the front and Gibson got out, giving the driver a quick wave as they left.

Piper stepped outside, waiting for him to reach her, a large duffle bag slung over one shoulder. "What's in there?" She gestured towards his bag.

"Some things I might find handy. Where does your friend live?"

She opened the foyer door. "In here."

Gibson followed her inside. "She lives in the same building as you?"

She led him to the elevator and gave Selene's floor number, hoping the elevator didn't take long to arrive. "No."

He chuckled. "Well, I can't say I blame you. I could be anyone. Zoe pretty much said the same thing about you. She thinks I'm an idiot for coming. Thinks this could be a set up."

She started to ask what he thought was a set up, but decided she had a more pressing question. "Why did you come?"

"I wanted to meet up with you earlier, remember?" He entered the elevator.

She followed him a second later. "I didn't forget."

"I thought you might have. I never heard back from you. Not even to tell me to stay away."

That was because she hadn't wanted to tell him to stay away, even though she knew she should. "I was thinking about it."

He grinned. "Does it always take you so long to make a decision?"

She was relieved when the elevator reached Selene's floor and the door opened. There was no way she wanted to answer that question. Normally she made her decisions far quicker than that.

He took hold of her arm, drawing her back to him after they'd stepped out of the elevator. "If you want me to take you inside your friend's apartment, you need to promise to listen and follow orders. It could be dangerous in there."

She shook her arm from his light grip. "I don't know if they're at home or out. I've knocked several times and no one has answered."

"That's not a problem."

She started to ask why not, but decided there was another question she wanted answered more. "Did you help any of the other people who called you?"

"Some."

"Why?"

"Because shutting ourselves away in the compound isn't going to make the problem go away."

Before she could ask about the compound, the elevator door opened again and several people stepped out. She waited for them to move off before she spoke. "Were you able to help them?"

"They didn't ask for help soon enough."

She nearly asked what he meant by that, but decided she really didn't want to know. At least not yet. "I don't have a key or a code to get inside Selene's place."

Gibson grinned. "As I said before, that's not a problem. Are you going to follow orders?"

She wanted to argue that it was wrong to break into someone's home, but she was too worried about Selene. "Okay." She led the way to the apartment, knocking on the door one more time. There was no answer.

Gibson placed his duffle bag on the floor at his feet, unzipping it. He drew out what looked like two pairs of white overalls, handing one to Piper.

She stared at the overalls she held while Gibson pulled on his. The material felt odd, like nothing she'd touched before. "What do we need these for?"

"Weren't you going to follow orders?"

She sent Gibson a glare before pulling on the overalls, muttering under her breath. They covered her from ankle to neck and out to her wrists. Once they were on, she followed Gibson's lead and drew up the drawstring hood, tightening the string. When he handed her some sort of breathing mask, she started to protest. His amused expression stopped her before she said a word. She watched how he put on his mask, covering his face, only his eyes and the area around them visible, before she pulled on the one he'd given her.

Gibson tightened the drawstrings at the wrists and

ankles of his overalls. "Make sure everything is sealed." He took out gloves and boot covers, pulling them on.

She tightened the strings on her overalls. "Why are we doing this?" She took the gloves and boot covers he handed her. They were made from the same material as the overalls.

"In case there are spores inside the apartment." He drew a small electronic item out of the duffle bag and attached it to the keypad of the door lock.

She was torn between asking him what he was using and wanting to argue about the spores. "Dawn can't make spores. The plants are infertile. They altered them so they couldn't reproduce." Her dad had said several times that the real reason was probably monetary. They wanted to continue charging an obscene price and there was no other way to control the market than to make the plants sterile.

The door swung open and Gibson met her gaze. "That's what they want you to think. And as long as the plants are given daily doses of the plant food they can't alter their DNA to return to normal."

"But-" She tried to think what to say. Her thoughts were a jumble. "Why would they risk it? All their reports say they're determined not to let her grow out of control and become a pest like so many other introduced species."

"Because they underestimated their abilities. They promised to have plants ready for sale and some of their backers are not the sort of people you disappoint. So they gambled that people would be more willing to follow care instructions carefully if the plants were rare and expensive." He paused a moment. "They obviously don't understand people." He drew a canister with a nozzle from the duffle bag. "They sold enough plants to keep their backers happy." Leaving the bag against the corridor wall, he stepped into the apartment.

Again Piper kept her comments to herself. As much as she wanted to argue, she had more important concerns. Like finding Selene. She followed Gibson, closing the door behind them and turning on the light. There was no one in the living room so she headed to Selene's bedroom. She stood in the doorway, staring at Dawn. Her mouth opened several times, but not a single word formed. Her thoughts were a bigger jumble and she took a single step forward.

Gibson pulled her back with a hand on her shoulder. "Don't take any chances. They mightn't have done the job properly." He entered the room, spraying the dead plant with his canister.

"What are you doing?" She watched the heavy white mist gush from the canister, leaving no visible residue behind.

"Freezing everything. Heat doesn't work to kill Dawns. Freezing also kills any spores in the air."

She stared at the splotches that dotted the surfaces, like splattered dandelion fluff. "Who did this?" She gestured vaguely around the room. "And where's Selene and her mum?"

Gibson glanced towards her, not bothering to answer before he crossed the room and looked out the window. He swore.

Chapter Ten

Piper crossed the room, trying to avoid the splatters that had once contained spores similar in size to specks of dust. Or so she'd learned from all she'd read about Dawn. "What's wrong?" She peered around him, trying to see what would have made him swear. Everything appeared normal. There were the pencil marks along the frame of the window, the window itself was open several centimetres and the only thing out of the ordinary were the splatters of spore carrying fluff on the window ledge. Thinking it might have been something Gibson had seen outside, she stared through the glass. Nothing. Everything was the same.

Gibson pointed to the splatters of fluff before sliding the window shut. "Some of it probably escaped."

"What has that got to do with where Selene is? All

I care about is finding my friend. That's why I asked you to come over here."

Gibson stared at her for nearly a minute before he spoke. "Do you know how the directors of the Dawn Project plan to break free from their more unsavoury backers? They've given them plants."

She took a step away from him, wondering if she could make it to the elevator before he stopped her. What she could see of his expression made her wonder about her safety. "How is that any different from all the plants they sold?"

"I'm not going to hurt you. And I'm not crazy. The directors gave their backers different plant food. They wanted Dawn to produce flowers as quickly as possible."

"You're as crazy as your father was." She regretted the words the moment she spoke them. A flicker of pain filled his eyes followed by anger. She didn't know whether to run or attack, but could see nothing to use against him. "I'm sorry, but what you said doesn't make sense. If the plants are dangerous why would they risk releasing them?" She kept backing away, wishing he'd stay still.

"People take risks they wouldn't normally take when their lives are at stake."

"According to you, letting Dawn out could risk

their lives anyway." She reached the doorway. Could she make it to the kitchen before he caught her? She glanced in that direction. Two sharp knives were kept in the second drawer.

"They have a plan. They'll steal back the plants they sold and destroy them. They thought the plant food would give them enough time to steal every Dawn without anyone suspecting them. And the backers live in an area that snows. They timed the release of the plants so that the snow will freeze the spores when they escape the warm environment of the dwellings."

"That is just-" she broke off, shaking her head. "Just-" No words came to mind. He was clearly insane. No wonder he hadn't recognised his father's insanity. Why had she called him? She should have deleted his message and never contacted him again.

"I know you have no reason to trust me, but you saw that in there." He gestured to the bedroom behind them. "How do you explain the dead plant and the disappearance of your friend?"

"Plants die." Not much further and she'd be in the kitchen. If she could keep him talking he mightn't do anything else. Like attack her. "What happened to the people you said you couldn't help? Why couldn't you help them?" She continued to back away.

Gibson continued to follow her. "Dawn grows fast."

His words confused her. "Did you find them?" She stepped into the kitchen. Now all she had to do was cross the room to the drawer. She glanced over her shoulder.

"Some of them didn't believe me straight away. Because of that the people they were looking for are already dead. Others didn't think to look for their friends and family until they'd been missing too long. Or put together the connection between the plant having flowered and the person going missing."

She breathed in sharply, stopping her slow backward steps. "Selene can't be dead." Another thought occurred to her. "Dawn hasn't been out in the public for long. It's only been nineteen days."

"Not everyone follows instructions. Some never gave their plants the food. We started getting calls four days after Dawn was sold. When did your friend fall sick?"

"Friday. It'll be a week tomorrow."

"Then you might be able to save her. I know where they take them."

About to take another step, she froze. What if he really did know? Just because he was crazy that didn't mean he knew nothing.

"But we have to leave. Before they arrive to deal with us. They're sure to have kept the place under surveillance."

There he went with the crazy comments again. How could she take him seriously when he kept making them? She met his gaze through the breathing mask. He didn't look crazy. Worried and sad. But that didn't mean he wasn't crazy. She didn't know what to do. Again she thought about the knives in the drawer that was only a couple of metres from her.

"What will it take to prove to you I'm speaking the truth?"

She didn't hesitate. "Finding my friend and her mum."

"Do they have a vehicle?"

She nodded, not sure how that was related to what she'd said.

"Okay. I'll show you where they are. Let's go back to the hallway and get cleaned up." He started to move away from her.

"Cleaned up?" With one last glance at the drawer, she followed him, keeping plenty of space between them. She doubted he'd be willing to help her if she brought the knives. Maybe she was the crazy one. But she had to see. Had to find out if he knew where

Selene was. He'd sounded so sincere. As crazy as his words were, he completely believed them.

He reached the front door and swung it open. "We don't want to risk inhaling any of the spore. It should be dead, but why take the chance? And what escaped would have already come to rest somewhere by now and have started growing."

Once he was out of the doorway, she stepped into the empty corridor with him. "How do we get cleaned up?"

Gibson closed the door. "Stretch your arms out to the side and I'll freeze any that might be on you." He pointed the nozzle of the canister at her.

She eyed the canister, not so sure it was a good idea. Although not much of the day had been. "What about you?"

"You'll have to do the same for me. Come on. Do you want to get caught?"

Of course she didn't, but she didn't know if someone was coming for them. Although she feared someone was coming. She'd seen that plant inside. As much as she wanted to believe her earlier comment of 'plants died', there'd been nothing natural about Dawn's death. If whatever was in that canister had caused it, what would it do to her? "That doesn't look safe."

"The overalls are made from a material with insulating properties." He paused. "Last chance. Do you want me to help you find your friend? I can't stay here any longer. It's not safe."

Hoping she didn't regret her choice, she held out her arms. At the last second, she closed her eyes. She heard the gush from the canister, but didn't feel anything. Opening her eyes, she saw Gibson step around behind her, continuing to spray her.

He stepped in front of her, holding out the canister. "My turn." He showed her how to make it work.

Feeling like she was in a bad dream, she sprayed Gibson and handed the canister back. After he returned it to his duffle bag, which had been left in the corridor, he removed his mask and protective gear. She did the same, following him to the elevator once everything was in the bag. None of this was what she'd expected when she'd agreed to meet him. Not that she knew what she'd expected. She'd been desperate and willing to take a chance that he might know what was happening. No one else seemed to have a clue. Nothing had changed. She was still desperate.

The trip to the ground floor was silent even though they had the elevator to themselves. When she would have left the apartment building, Gibson put a hand on her arm, drawing her back.

"Wait a minute." He sent a message on his communication device.

"What are we waiting for?"

"Zoe."

"Your sister?"

He nodded. "She'll pick us up."

She wanted to protest that she wasn't about to get into a vehicle with him and his sister, but she spotted Linda coming out of the stairwell and head to the elevator. Linda hadn't looked in their direction yet. "We have to go." She kept her voice quiet as she tugged Gibson towards the front door. Linda must have become impatient waiting for the elevator to reach the underground parking garage and taken the stairs to the foyer. It wasn't the first time. Linda had tried to get her and Selene to use the stairs more than once. They'd preferred to wait.

Gibson followed her outside. "What's wrong?"

"Linda has arrived." She checked her communication device, surprised more time had passed than she'd expected.

"Who?"

"Selene's aunt. Evelyn's sister." She thought of the

mess in the apartment. "Will it be safe in there for her?"

Gibson shrugged. "It should be, but I can't guarantee anything."

Chapter Eleven

Piper was tempted to run back inside to tell Linda, but doubted she'd believe her. How could she convince anyone that Gibson was telling the truth when she wasn't certain he was? She was only going with him because she didn't want to take the risk he was telling the truth and knew where Selene was and something happened to her best friend because she didn't check out the flimsy lead.

The same vehicle that had dropped Gibson off earlier pulled up in front of them. He took her arm. "Let's get out of here."

She got in the back seat, hoping she wasn't making a mistake. But what else could she do? Selene had been missing for nearly a week.

Zoe glanced towards her. "Why are you bringing her? She could be working for them."

"They've been in there. I found a dead plant."

"Did you wear the protective gear? Did you freeze any spores that were left lying around? Is the site contained?" Zoe pulled out into the traffic with a glance over her shoulder.

"I do know what I'm doing, Zoe."

"That's what Dad thought too."

Gibson rested his hand on Zoe's shoulder. "He didn't know what we now know."

Zoe shrugged him off. "Whatever."

Piper glanced outside, looking behind at the disappearing apartment building. Her mouth dropped open when a man entered. He looked like the one who'd given her and Selene the creeps. It had to be the distance. There was no way it was him again. She faced forward. "Where are we going?"

"How would I know? I'm just the driver," Zoe muttered.

"Dawn Project Lab."

"Are you crazy?"

Zoe looked at her brother long enough that Piper wanted to tell her to keep her eyes on the road. "Why are we going there?" She'd always wanted to visit the lab, but not like this.

"That's where they'll have taken your friend." Gibson turned from Piper to Zoe. "I'm not planning on going inside. We need to get close enough we can use the VE to see what vehicles are in their parking lot."

Piper stared at him. They had Vision Enhancers? That was military equipment. Something she'd only seen in movies. She was beginning to regret leaving the knives behind.

"I'm going to be really annoyed with you if you get me killed," Zoe muttered.

Piper had to agree with her. "How will going to the lab help?" Not that she wanted to enter the lab with them, but if he believed Selene and Evelyn were inside, how else could he prove it?

"Are you sure you'll recognise Evelyn's vehicle?"

She nodded.

"Then it'll help."

"This is a bad idea," Zoe muttered.

Gibson smiled. "Have a little faith. I do know what I'm doing, Zoe."

"You better call Jerome and make sure he isn't planning anything crazy," Zoe said. "And put it on speaker so I know what's going on."

Gibson took out his communication device.

While he waited for Jerome to answer, Piper wondered if she should let her parents know where she was. It only took her a few seconds to decide that was a crazy idea. They'd demand she return home and she'd never know for certain if Gibson knew where Selene was. Although it probably wasn't as crazy as getting in a vehicle with two people she didn't know.

Jerome finally answered. "What's up, Gib?"

"We're heading out to do a visual of the Dawn Project Lab. Just want to make sure we won't be getting in your way," Gibson said.

"Don't tell me you're finally going to do something practical."

Gibson shook his head, even though it wasn't a video call. "We're only taking a look."

"If you change your mind, we're heading over there tomorrow night to cause a bit of havoc."

"Be careful," Zoe said.

"The same goes for you two. They've taken enough lives without giving them any more. Let me know if you see anything interesting."

"Okay. We will." Gibson disconnected the call.

"Who was that?" Piper asked.

"One of the scientists that helped my father smuggle out a piece of Dawn so they could carry out some independent tests," Gibson said.

"You didn't think we were in this on our own, did you?" Zoe asked. "We have people that would look for us if we went missing."

She wanted to say the same. Wanted to warn Zoe that if anything happened to her, then her parents would look for her. But how could they? As far as they knew, she was at Selene's place. "All I'm interested in is finding my friend."

Gibson turned in his seat to look at her. "Jerome is one of the five scientists that helped our father try and prove that Dawn isn't safe. There's only two of them left."

"Why does he hate Dawn so much?" She could understand why these two hated the plants. They believed Dawn had killed their father.

Gibson stared at her for a moment. "His wife was one of the scientists. Dawn killed Macie and nearly killed him too."

She couldn't continue to meet his gaze. Not without wanting to argue. Did he know how crazy he sounded? She looked out the window, trying to think what else to say. There was nothing. Not without upsetting them. Maybe it'd be best to remain silent. She'd see if they knew where Selene was and then go home. If Selene and Evelyn were at the Dawn Project Laboratory she'd tell her parents and the police. But she doubted they'd be there. She just didn't want to be left wondering.

Before they reached the laboratory, Piper received

a call from her mum. She answered it without video. The last thing she needed was for them to find out exactly where she was. "Hello."

"Where are you? Linda said you weren't over there."

"I ran into a friend who said they thought they'd seen Selene recently. I'm checking."

"What friend. And where are you going?"

"We're arriving now. I'll call you when I find out for certain. I won't be long." She had no idea how far they were from the lab, but it was all she could think to say.

"Piper–"

She disconnected the call and turned off the communication device. Sighing heavily, she returned it to her pocket. She was going to be in so much trouble when she got home.

"Problems?" Zoe asked.

Piper didn't like the tone Zoe used. As if she was laughing at her. "Not at all. They'll get over it." She shrugged, trying not to think about how long she was likely to be grounded.

It took them nearly an hour to reach their destination. When Zoe pulled up, Piper got out of the vehicle to stand beside Gibson. He held out the Visual Enhancers and pointed to the buildings sprawled in the middle of the large parking lot below them. Taking them, Piper walked to the edge of the roadside, stepping over the guardrail that separated the weedy edge from the rocky ground that dropped away to a steep hillside.

Zoe came to stand beside her. "We haven't got all day."

Before Piper could say anything, Gibson joined them. "Don't pressure her. It's a lot to take in."

Tuning out Zoe's angry reply, she brought the Visual Enhancers to her eyes. Looking through them, she pressed a button on the side, the image going strange. She pressed the button several more times, cycling through the different views until she'd returned to daytime function. She had no idea what most of the functions were, only knowing there would be at least heat and night vision. She checked the side of the Visual Enhancers so that this time when she brought them back up she was able to press the correct button and zoom in on the parking lot. It was probably a waste of time, but she wanted to look anyway. Most of the vehicles were white, which didn't make it easy when looking for a white vehicle. She stared at row upon row until they started to look the same. Then she saw it. She took the Visual Enhancers away from her eyes and stared at the spot they'd been trained on. Surely she was mistaken. Once more she brought them to her eyes to stare at the vehicle.

"You found it, didn't you?"

Lowering the Visual Enhancers, she faced Gibson, noticing Zoe was no longer with them. A glance showed she was beside the vehicle. "Maybe…" She couldn't think of another explanation. "It can't be…" Again her voice trailed off. None of it could be real. The words and images from Kyndall's website came to mind. No. That couldn't happen to Selene. She wasn't going to let Selene's lungs be destroyed by Dawn, her last hours spent gasping for breath. She held out the Visual Enhancers, slowly shaking her head, fighting the urge to back away from him and the pity in his eyes.

"I'm sorry. I know how you feel."

Piper shook her head. "You don't." How could he, when she didn't know? Her emotions were a jumble. She alternated between horror and disbelief.

"My father." The words were whisper quiet.

"Will they help her?" She gestured towards the laboratory, her gaze remaining on Gibson as she mentally begged him to say yes.

"No. And not because they don't want to. Their drugs are in the experimental phase too."

"Too?"

"Ours aren't much better."

He was saying Selene was going to die? "We don't know if Selene is in there. It might only be her mum."

"Then where is she?"

She couldn't answer. Turning away, she headed for the vehicle.

"What are you planning on doing?"

She stepped over the guardrail before facing him. "What can I do?"

It was Zoe who answered. "Rescue her."

Chapter Twelve

Piper stared at Zoe, not sure if she was serious. "How?"

Zoe's lips curved into a smile. There was nothing reassuring about it. "We join Jerome tomorrow night."

"No." Gibson stepped over the guardrail to stand close to his sister. "Dad would be appalled."

"Dad's not here." Zoe spat out the words. "He's dead." Her hand made a sweeping gesture towards the laboratory. "It's their fault." Zoe turned to Piper. "Do you want a lift home? I can pick you up tomorrow night if you want to get your friend back."

"No, I mean yes, but I can't go home. Not if I want to go with you tomorrow night." After leaving her device turned off this long there was no doubt she'd be grounded.

"Where do you want me to drop you?"

Piper shrugged. She didn't have a clue.

"She could come back to the compound," Gibson said.

Zoe's eyes narrowed. "No way. I don't trust her."

"Then why did you invite her to join you tomorrow night? Aren't you afraid she'll tell someone?"

"No. I'll have Jerome monitor her device." Zoe looked towards Piper. "And if she tries anything tomorrow night, I'll shoot her."

It took all Piper's willpower not to step back from the venomous look Zoe gave her. What had happened to make the girl hate the world and everything in it? The website came to mind and she felt like an idiot. Kyndall. And Dawn. It was meant to be the discovery of a lifetime.

"She's coming to the compound." Gibson's tone was firm.

"I'm not about to let you get me killed because you're interested in some girl. If you get yourself killed, that's your problem." Zoe strode to the vehicle and took off before either of them had a chance to move.

Piper stared after the disappearing vehicle. "What do we do now?"

Gibson sat on the edge of the guardrail. "Wait."

Piper eyed him up and down, trying to make sense of his comment. She doubted public transport came out this way. "What are we waiting for?"

"Zoe."

She looked between Gibson and the direction the vehicle had disappeared in. "She's gone."

Gibson grinned, patting the top of the guardrail beside him. "Take a seat. It'll probably take awhile for her to cool down."

"She's coming back?" Piper took several steps towards Gibson.

"Yeah. Eventually."

He didn't look like it bothered him. Actually, nothing his sister had done appeared to have bothered him. Not even Zoe saying he was interested in her. She wondered if that was because he wasn't really and his sister had been trying to annoy him. "What if she doesn't come back?"

"She will." He patted the guardrail beside him again. "It's perfectly safe to sit next to me." He grinned. "What are you worried about?"

Absolutely everything. Instead of saying that, she sat beside him leaving plenty of space between them, trying to think of a way to change the topic. Her worries weren't up for discussion. "You said there were two of the six scientists left who smuggled

Dawn out of the lab." She couldn't resist a glance over her shoulder towards the laboratory.

"Yeah. Jerome and Emerson."

"Is he helping Jerome?"

Gibson shook his head. "No, he's been staying with us. He doesn't believe violence is the answer. He's trying to find a cure."

"Will he be able to help Selene?"

"Probably not. None of the lab rats have lived."

"What do you mean? What lab rats?"

"The ones we expose to the spore. You don't think we're like them, do you?" He gestured towards the laboratory. "We don't use humans to test the drugs."

Her stomach lurched and she rose to her feet, backing away from Gibson, shaking her head. "No. They don't. Tell me they're not experimenting on Selene and Evelyn."

Gibson rose to his feet and reached for her, his mouth opening. He let his arm fall to his side and closed his mouth, turning away from her. He was silent for nearly a minute. "I'm sorry. I hadn't planned to say that."

She crossed the distance between them, grabbing his arm and turning him to face her. "They aren't experimenting on Selene."

He remained silent, staring down at her.

She shook his arm that she continued to hold. "I mean it."

"Piper–"

"No." She didn't like the tone of voice he was using.

"I'm sorry. I'll come with you if you want. Tomorrow night. But only if you plan to go in, get your friend and leave straight away. No revenge."

Before she could answer, she heard an approaching vehicle. Turning her head, she saw it was Zoe. She let go of Gibson and faced the road, relieved she didn't need to answer immediately.

Zoe pulled up and stepped out of the vehicle, her arms crossing over her chest. "You can come with us to our place only if you give me your device. I'm not letting anyone use it to track you down."

"It's not on."

Zoe held out her hand. "I don't care. You could turn it back on."

Piper continued to meet Zoe's hazel eyes. They might have been identical in colour to her brother's, but they were lacking the calmness and compassion that were in his. All she could see in Zoe's eyes was anger and distrust. Were they some of the emotions Zoe could see in her eyes?

"Well?"

Not wanting Zoe to drive off again, Piper handed over the communication device. It wasn't like she planned to use it any time soon. Not until after she'd found Selene. "You will return it when we leave your place." She made it a statement, not a question.

Zoe nodded before getting in the vehicle.

When everyone was buckled up, Zoe drove towards the city. Piper was relieved the drive was silent. She didn't feel like talking to anyone. All she wanted was to find Selene. What if waiting an entire night was too long? That would make it a week since Selene had disappeared. And what would her parents do when she returned home? She was going to be grounded for life. Not that it mattered if everything on Kyndall's website was true.

The questions continued to tumble around in her mind, not a single answer appearing. She was almost relieved when they turned down a narrow dirt road before reaching the city and went through a tunnel of overgrown trees and shrubs. Relief was followed by fear. "Where are you taking me?" The deserted, hidden road made her think of serial killers, shallow graves and a painful death.

"I was wondering when you were going to stop sulking about me taking your device."

"I wasn't sulking. I was thinking. Where are you taking me?"

"The compound." Gibson turned in his seat to face her. "It's actually our father's lab. They trashed our house so we had to hide out here."

"Who did?"

"You're not very smart, are you?" Zoe asked.

Gibson answered before Piper could say anything to Zoe. "People from the Dawn Project."

She had other questions to ask, but decided to wait until Zoe wasn't around. Without her comments she might actually get some answers.

Zoe pulled up in front of a fine mesh gate, the top of it not visible through the greenery. She waited, her hands tapping impatiently. "He better not be expecting me to get out and put in the code. He said he'd let us in," she muttered. When the gates swung open, she drove forward. "Finally."

Piper noticed a keypad as they drove in the gates. Ahead of them was another mesh gate and Piper turned to watch the first one close, trapping them in a cage like area. Nozzles along the side of the cage gushed a heavy white mist at the vehicle. "What's going on?"

"We're making sure no spores are being brought

into our place. We don't want to contaminate our environment," Gibson said.

When the mist disappeared and the gates in front of them opened, Zoe drove forward and parked next to the closest building. She opened her door, facing Piper before she got out. "If you try and hurt us, or trick us, I will kill you." She left the vehicle, not waiting for a reply.

Piper stared after Zoe as she headed towards a cluster of three buildings, the middle one larger than the other two.

"She takes a little getting used to."

Piper turned her gaze to Gibson. "A little?" She didn't bother keeping the disbelief from her voice.

Gibson grinned. "Yep. Only a little." He got out of the vehicle, waiting for her to join him.

Chapter Thirteen

Piper took a deep breath before she joined Gibson. Slowly turning, she looked around the compound. The area was bigger than she expected, the mesh going overhead so they were in a completely enclosed cage. Above them was a single mesh, not the double one they'd entered. The outer fence had saplings pressed up against it in places, keeping them and the shrubs back from the inner mesh. Each roof of the buildings contained rows of solar tiles and she caught a glimpse of a smaller building behind the larger one, possibly several more, but it was difficult to tell from where she stood. The building she could see, appeared to be a greenhouse. What kind of lab was this? She took another deep breath, trying to force away the fear that threatened to strike. "Now what?"

"Do you want to meet Emerson?"

"I don't know? Is he likely to want to threaten me too?"

Gibson chuckled, slinging an arm around her shoulders. "Come on. You'll like him."

She wasn't so certain about that, but let Gibson guide her in the direction Zoe had taken. When they entered the building, Piper looked around the large room that was filled with laboratory equipment. Zoe stood talking to a man that looked about thirty. He wore a white lab coat that seemed almost dark against his pallid skin. His blue eyes kept looking everywhere, as if expecting something to jump out and grab him.

Zoe glared at them. "The entire world is screwed. I'll let him tell you about it." She strode from the building.

Gibson sighed. "What's wrong, Emerson?"

"Their plan failed."

"You're going to have to be a little clearer than that. Whose plan? And what plan?" Gibson's arm remained around Piper's shoulders.

She wasn't sure if she should step away from Gibson. With the wild look in Emerson's eyes it was probably safer not to make any sudden movements.

"The directors of the Dawn Project. Some of their

backers survived. They're out for blood. Especially since the plants killed numerous family members."

Gibson groaned. "Everyone is dead. The directors have started a world war."

She really needed more information to make sense of what was going on. "Why? Won't the backers only go after the directors?"

"Yes, but there are always casualties. And it's usually the innocent."

Gibson's words made Piper think of Selene. There was no way she wanted her friend to be a casualty. "Will this change Jerome's plans?"

"I don't know. I better get in touch with him."

"You're not helping Jerome, are you?" Emerson demanded.

"No, we're making the most of his distraction to rescue Piper's friend." Gibson looked from one to the other. "Piper, meet Emerson. Emerson, this is Piper. Her friend is at the Dawn Project Lab. And I'm guessing she didn't go there willingly."

Piper smiled weakly, not sure what to say. 'I'm pleased to meet you' didn't seem like the right comment under the circumstances.

"Don't let Jerome talk you into anything. Don't break your promise to your father."

"I wasn't planning to." Gibson turned to Piper.

"Come on." He guided her outside and headed for one of the smaller buildings.

"Where are we going?"

"My place." He held the door open and stepped back to let her through.

Piper reluctantly moved away from him, wondering at her sanity. She didn't know him and shouldn't trust him. Entering the cottage, she stopped just inside. She was in a small, open plan kitchen and living area with three other doors leading out of the room.

Gibson pointed to each of the doors. "Bedroom, bathroom, study."

"This is your place? You don't share it with anyone?"

"All mine. Dad built this compound using the money they framed him with. He wanted a safe place for us when everything went wrong. Jerome has a similar set up. Although his place is more military looking with dorms and everything."

She could only shake her head. The day kept getting stranger. When Gibson took out his communication device, she remembered Zoe's earlier words. "Put it on speaker so I know what's going on." She was relieved when he did.

"What's up, Gib?" Jerome asked.

"The backers–"

"I've already heard."

"Does this change your plans?"

Piper hoped it didn't. She had no idea how they'd rescue Selene without help.

"We're discussing that. I'll let you know when we figure it out," Jerome said.

"Okay. I'll wait to hear from you." Gibson ended the call. "I'll send Zoe a message to let her know." Once that was done, he returned his communication device to his pocket. "Are you hungry?" He gestured towards the kitchen.

She shook her head. There was no way she'd be able to eat until she knew what was happening. She wasn't about to leave Selene or Evelyn at the Dawn Project Laboratory. They weren't lab rats that could be experimented on. Anger rushed through her and she began to worry Gibson had been right to tell her there'd be no revenge. She'd never felt so angry before in her life.

Gibson gestured towards the couch. "You want to watch something?"

It took a few seconds for his words to sink in. "The news." Maybe there'd be something on it about what was happening.

"Okay."

They scoured the different channels for several hours, taking a break when Gibson said he was hungry even if she wasn't. Piper joined him for dinner, picking at her food. It wasn't until they were again watching the news that Jerome called.

"Can you be ready in an hour? We're going tonight."

"Where do we meet you?"

"I'll send you a location for the team you'll go in with. How many of you are going?"

Piper nodded when Gibson looked in her direction. He wasn't leaving her behind. The thought of entering the lab terrified her, but not as much as the thought of losing her friend.

"Two. Possibly three."

"I'll send a message shortly." Jerome ended the call.

Gibson rose from the couch. "I'll let Zoe know. Do you want to come with me?"

She managed not to say, 'do you think I'm stupid?' shaking her head instead.

"I won't be long."

When she was alone, Piper rose to her feet, wondering what she should do. How did one get ready to break into a heavily guarded laboratory? She momentarily closed her eyes. Zoe wasn't the only crazy person around this place. Or maybe the craziness was catching. She thought of the wild look in Emerson's eyes. She really hoped not. The sound of the door opening had her spinning to face it, her heart racing.

Zoe walked into the room ahead of Gibson. "Remember what I said." She pointed a warning finger at Piper.

Gibson pushed Zoe's arm down. "You ready, Piper?"

No, she wasn't close to ready. She nodded instead of speaking. There was no way she was about to let that word escape. Not with Zoe glaring at her and the words the girl had spoken earlier ringing in her mind. 'If you try and hurt us or trick us, I will kill you.' She didn't doubt Zoe would follow through on her threat.

It was after midnight when they arrived at the location Jerome had sent them. They'd dressed in protective gear, like the five people waiting for them, a balaclava hiding their faces and most of their breathing masks too. There were three men and two women, all carrying various weapons. Ones that looked like something soldiers would carry.

For what felt like the millionth time, Piper wondered what she was doing here. What if Selene and Evelyn weren't in the laboratory? Even worse, what if they were caught breaking in? And what had made her think getting involved with a fanatical, gun carrying group was a good idea?

"If we run into trouble, you kids stay out of the way," one of the men said.

Gibson nodded, shushing Zoe with a motion of his hand.

"All right then. Stay in the middle of the group and follow orders." The man led the way, a woman and a man with him, the other two bringing up the rear.

Piper wondered who they were. No one had exchanged names. Was that typical? Were they meant to remain anonymous? She didn't have a clue. Pretty much like everything else these days. She was sick of being clueless. Things weren't meant to go like this. She'd been so excited. It was hard to believe that twenty days ago she'd thought life couldn't get much better. That only owning a Dawn could have improved it.

They reached the outer perimeter and the man held up his hand to halt. Piper stared at the mesh fence, wondering what they were waiting for. Eventually the man gave the order to cut the wire and one of the men used bolt cutters to do the job. They streamed through the gap in single file, silently crossing the parking lot.

There were too many lights for Piper's liking. It

felt like everyone could see her. She guessed people could. Or at least she was probably on the security footage. Was this the group that had attacked the Dawn Project Laboratory last time? A shudder ran through her. They'd caused so much damage. What did they plan to do this time?

Chapter Fourteen

She heard shouts and the sound of weapons being fired. The group she was with sprinted towards the buildings and she raced after them, not wanting to be left behind. They came to a stop at one of the entrances and the leader pulled out a small electronic item to use on the keypad beside the door.

Sirens sounded and Piper couldn't stop looking around, heart racing, fighting the urge to run back the way they'd come. She kept expecting something to go wrong. The police to grab them or one of them to be shot. The door swung open and the leader checked inside before waving them through. Piper cautiously entered the building. Selene better be in here after going through all this. Then she immediately hoped she wasn't since that meant she was dying. Although if she wasn't here, then where was she? She had no idea which was the best scenario.

Neither of them appealed to her. As was becoming common lately, her thoughts were a jumble and she had no idea what to think.

When they reached an intersection in the corridor they ran along, the leader held up his hand to halt. Then held up four fingers, pointing to the left. The two in the lead with him nodded, the man crouching near the edge of the wall.

The woman nodded and held out her gun, running across the intersecting corridor, firing. She pressed herself against the wall on the other side, waiting for the return fire to finish.

Piper watched as the three of them peered around the corner, firing again. The other two remained behind them, watching for anyone who might enter the building and attack from the rear. Shouts, sirens and gunfire filled the building. What had made her think she could do this? She was a kid, still in school. An image of Selene filled her mind. Fear raced through her at the thought of losing her friend, greater than the fear she already felt. She had to find Selene.

"Move," the leader ordered.

Piper couldn't resist looking as they crossed the intersecting corridor. Four bodies slumped on the floor brought her to a stop. They'd killed them?

Gibson slipped his hand in hers, tugging her forward. "They're not dead. He uses tranquillisers."

"Who?"

"No names in here, but you know who I'm talking about."

She guessed he meant Jerome.

"Hurry up," the leader ordered.

They reached the end of the corridor and turned left. Partway along they paused at a right turn. The leader held up a hand as he peered around the corner. He pulled back, leaning against the wall and frowned. "The order came through to pull out. There's another team on the way. Heavily armed ground and aerial forces. Estimated arrival is five to ten minutes. I guess the backers are ready to strike. We've lost our opportunity."

"What? No. I can't leave. My friend's in here somewhere," Piper protested.

"If we don't leave now, we could get caught between two forces," the leader said.

"We're nearly there. They keep them in the room at the end of this corridor." The man at the rear gestured towards the corridor they were about to enter.

"We don't have time. What if we run into more

patrols? Move out. Now." The leader headed back the way they'd come.

Piper looked between him and the corridor that led to Selene. She couldn't go. Mentally crossing her fingers, she dashed into the corridor and ran towards the end. Behind her she heard the sound of footsteps, shouts to come back and orders to forget about her. Reaching the door at the end of the corridor, she flung it open.

"I'm going to kill you." Zoe came to a stop at her shoulder.

Piper glanced behind and saw Gibson was with them too. Ignoring Zoe's comment, she forced herself to enter the room. On a stainless steel bench was something that looked very much like what should be found inside a person, not be dissected on a bench. What looked like fine white hairs was threaded through it and she tried not to think about what it had once been.

"That's what Dawn does to your lungs. Do you want a plant now?" Zoe demanded.

Piper swallowed hard, wishing Zoe hadn't told her exactly what she was looking at. It had been better when she hadn't known for certain. She stepped around a glass display case that contained a large Dawn surrounded by dandelion like fluff. She froze, spying three figures lying on stainless steel benches. One of them was Selene. Her legs felt like jelly as she staggered forward, resting a hand on Selene's shoulder when she reached her side.

"Get her unhooked so we can get out of here." Zoe started removing cords from Selene's arm and temple.

"What?" Why was Zoe bothering? Selene was clearly dead. No one could be that white and live.

"She's alive. Sedated, but alive." Gibson pushed her gently aside to help Zoe.

Piper couldn't move. Her friend was alive? It didn't seem possible. She looked dead, like the other two people did. Gibson gave Selene an injection, about to join Zoe who was unhooking the other two, when Piper grabbed hold of his arm.

"What did you do to her?"

"It'll counteract the sedation. We can't carry her out of here. Give her a few seconds and she'll start to wake." He pulled away from Piper to join Zoe.

Piper pressed a hand against Selene's chest, trying to find a heartbeat. For a moment she thought there was none and then she found it. "Selene." She grabbed her friend's shoulders and tried to draw her up. "Selene, wake up. Please." How long should the injection take? It had been more than a few seconds. Was she worse than Gibson had thought?

Selene's eyes fluttered open. "Piper?" Selene looked around the room, her gaze eventually returning to Piper. "How did you find me? Why are you wearing that outfit?"

"I'll tell you later. Where's your mum?"

Tears welled up in Selene's eyes. "They killed her. She had a bad reaction to the drugs." She choked back a sob. "When they gave them to me, I thought I was dead too."

"Come on. We've got to get out of here." Gibson supported a young man, his skin unnaturally white compared to his black hair.

"It's too late for this one." Zoe moved away from the woman on the last bench. "We've got to run. It's getting noisy out there."

They were halfway across the room when three people burst in, firing a spray of bullets. Piper dragged Selene to the floor as the glass display case shattered and the dandelion like fluff filled the air. Seeing Gibson and Zoe run in a crouch to the nearest stainless steel bench, she did the same, dragging Selene with her. The young man lay face down on the floor and she didn't know if he lived.

Gunfire sounded again and as soon as it stopped, Zoe drew a gun and popped up long enough to fire a couple of times. She crouched against the stainless steel bench waiting for the gunfire to finish before she attacked again.

Piper stared at Zoe, not having expected her to draw a weapon. Did she use tranquillisers too?

After the third time, Zoe remained standing. "They're down. Let's get moving."

Piper helped Selene to her feet and walked around the bench. Gibson followed, supporting the young man. Zoe ran ahead of them, the gun out as she peered around the doorframe. Piper had nearly passed the third figure sprawled on the floor when they reached out and grabbed her ankle, tripping her. Selene went sprawling across the floor with her.

The figure wrestled with her and she saw he had a knife. He grabbed at her breathing mask and balaclava, pulling them off a moment before Zoe shot him.

Gibson dropped the man he was helping, running towards her. "Don't breathe. Whatever you do, don't breathe."

Holding her breath, she reached for the mask.

"No. You can't use that. Come on. We have to get you out of here." Gibson helped her to her feet.

"You pair run ahead. I've got these two." Zoe gestured towards the young man and Selene with her gun.

Piper wanted to argue, but she couldn't do that and hold her breath. Gibson dragged her to the door.

"Hurry." His voice was urgent.

She ran beside him, already wanting to take a breath.

As if he knew, Gibson said, "Don't breathe. Whatever you do, don't breathe."

Dark spots danced at the edge of her vision and she stumbled at the panic she heard in his voice. He threw her over his shoulder, her face near his stomach and his hand clamped over her nose and mouth. Her vision dimmed and sound faded. The next thing she knew someone was shaking her hard.

"Piper."

She heard fear in Gibson's voice and she opened her eyes to see his shadowy figure leaning over her. "Selene? Where's Selene?" She struggled to sit up.

"I'm here."

With Gibson's help, Piper sat up and saw Selene lying in the dirt not far from her. She glanced around, trying to figure out where they were. Zoe stood nearby, a gun in her hand, and the young man was hunched over. His legs were drawn up to rest his head on. Beyond them the sky was filled with fire and the sound of fighting reached her. "Where are we?"

"Not far enough away," Zoe said.

"Can you walk?" Gibson continued to stare at her, his breathing mask on, the balaclava now off.

Piper nodded even though she felt shaky and light headed. They obviously couldn't stay here. Not with the sound of fighting nearby.

Gibson offered her his hand, and when she was standing, put an arm around her waist. "Are you okay?"

She wasn't sure, but nodded anyway. She tried not to think about what had happened, but images continued to flash through her mind. The man dragging her breathing mask off, dandelion like fluff floating around her and the fear in Gibson's eyes.

Selene struggled to her feet and Gibson turned to hold out a hand, continuing to hold onto Piper. "Can you walk? We don't have far to go."

Selene shrugged. "Where are we going? Will they find us?" Selene looked back in the direction of the fire. No one answered her.

Zoe led the way, the young man stumbling beside her. "You're not getting in my vehicle. All of you are contaminated."

"We can deal with that," Gibson said.

Piper hoped so. She wasn't about to leave anyone behind.

When they reached the vehicle, Gibson sprayed

Piper, Selene and the young man with pressurised air while Zoe stood behind them with the canister to freeze any spores that came off them. Gibson and Zoe then took turns at spraying each other with the freezing mist. They gave Piper, Selene and the young man medical masks to wear.

"Wear it," Zoe ordered when Piper didn't put hers on.

"What is it for?" She stared at the white fabric of the mask.

"To catch any spores you might breathe out."

"I'm not infected," Piper stated.

Zoe glared at her, gesturing towards Selene and the young man. "They certainly are infected. Probably far enough along the plant is producing new spores for them to breathe out. Spores you might have breathed in even if you didn't breathe in any at the lab. You might not be infected, but I'm not taking that chance. You want to get in my vehicle, you'll wear it."

Gibson took the mask from Piper. "It's a precaution. Nothing more. You didn't breathe in any of the spores."

Chapter Fifteen

Piper let Gibson slip the mask on her, hearing in his voice that he didn't believe a word he said. She watched as Gibson and Zoe removed their protective gear. The images rushed through her mind again, the one of the dandelion like fluff lingering. She couldn't be infected. The image of lungs filled with white threads joined the images of spores. Closing her eyes didn't help.

"Get in the vehicle if you're coming with us." Zoe sat in the driver's seat. "I'm not waiting around for anyone."

Piper waited until they were in the vehicle before she spoke. "What happened to everyone else?"

"They weren't stupid enough to stick around." Starting the vehicle, Zoe glanced over her shoulder to Piper who sat in the back between Selene and the young man they'd rescued. "I told you not to try and get us killed. What were you thinking?"

"Would you have left Gibson there?" Piper felt a grim satisfaction when Zoe didn't answer.

"Where are you taking us?" the young man asked.

"I have no idea." Zoe glanced towards Gibson as she drove away from the laboratory. "And you better not say the compound. I'm not about to let them contaminate it when they die."

Piper heard Selene's sharply indrawn breath and wanted to hit Zoe. Since the girl was the one driving she managed to control the impulse. "They're not going to die. None of us are."

"Why? Because you say so?"

Piper ignored Zoe's mocking tone. "What did Jerome and Emerson do differently to everyone else who died?"

"Nothing. They both took the same drugs as the others. And the same dose worked out according to their weight," Zoe said.

"There has to be something." Piper looked from Zoe to Gibson, wanting to demand he tell her a different answer.

"You can read the notes they kept," Gibson said.

"We are not taking them to the compound."

Gibson continued talking, as if his sister hadn't

spoken. "Emerson has gone over the doses hundreds of times. There's nothing different. He also couldn't see any genetic differences that would have helped."

"Are you listening to me?" Zoe demanded.

Gibson met her gaze before she returned to watching the road. "Take them to the compound. Emerson can check them over to make sure they're not bugged."

"Bugged?" There was a high pitch to Selene's voice.

Hoping to prevent her friend from becoming hysterical, Piper turned to the young man beside her, holding out her hand. "I'm Piper." She introduced the rest of the people in the vehicle.

He shook her hand. "Wyatt."

"How did they get you?" Selene leaned forward so she could see Wyatt past Piper. "Were you stupid enough to go to a hospital too?"

He shook his head. "My family did. I came home to find the place empty and that fluff everywhere. The air felt like it burned my lungs. I called out to them, but no one answered. Not my two older brothers and not my parents. The apartment was empty. I'd barely shut the front door and spotted a note from my parents to say they were at the hospital when guys in hazmat suits came bursting in, spraying everything with their canisters. One of them pointed a gun at me and I thought I was dead. Next thing I remember is waking up in a lab, half out of it."

Silence filled the vehicle and Piper tried to think of a way to break it.

"Where are we taking them?" Zoe asked again.

"I already told you," Gibson said.

"She's not worth dying over," Zoe muttered.

"Zoe." There was a warning in Gibson's voice.

"Fine. But you're an idiot. Until Emerson says they're clear, they stay in quarantine and you stay away from the three of them. Do you want to die too?"

"I'm not infected." Piper tried not to let the fear she felt colour her words, but she was unsuccessful.

"You need to stay in quarantine until we find out if you breathed in any of the spore. It doesn't take much," Zoe said. "A single dust particle. And then you're dead."

She hadn't breathed any of it in. She was certain. But what about when she'd been unconscious? And when they'd been outside, before Gibson had sprayed them down. She wanted to go home. Wanted to talk to her parents and tell them what was happening, in case she didn't get another chance to speak to them ever again.

Selene took hold of her hand, wrapping it tightly between hers. "Thank you for coming after me."

Piper nodded.

"Thanks for not leaving me behind," Wyatt said. "I can't believe I'm alive."

"Won't be for much longer," Zoe muttered.

Piper wanted to yell at her, but guessed it would be a waste of effort. "Can I have my device? I need to call my parents."

"At this hour?" Zoe asked. "They'll probably be asleep."

"I doubt it. Now where is it?" Piper took it when Zoe handed it through. "Can we pull over? I need to get out for a few minutes." She didn't want anyone listening in on her conversation. There was a distinct possibility she'd burst into tears and begin crying messily.

"Oh, come on. Seriously?" Zoe asked.

"Pull over," Gibson said.

While Zoe pulled over onto the side of the road, Piper turned the communication device on. She ignored the missed calls and numerous messages, waiting until she could climb out over Selene before she called her mum. She walked away from the vehicle, trying not to cry when she heard her mum's voice. She had to remain calm. Her mum wouldn't be able to understand her if she cried.

"Where are you? Do you know how worried we've been?"

"I'm sorry." She cleared her throat, trying to focus on what she had to say. "I don't have much time." She doubted Zoe would stick around for long. "I found Selene."

"You did? Where are you? Linda is frantic. What about Evelyn?"

"She's dead. Look, I know you'll have lots of questions, but I don't have time for all of them. Dawn isn't the plant we expected. They lied to us. She's a killer."

"Piper–"

She cut off her mum's hesitant voice. "I know I sound crazy. I'm sorry. I broke into the Dawn Project Laboratory and helped Selene escape. People were trying to kill us." Her voice shook and she took a steadying breath. It didn't help, only made her think of breathing in spores.

"Where are you? We'll come and get you. Both of you."

She could hear it in her mum's voice that she didn't believe a word she spoke. "I can't come home. I might be infected too. I'm sorry."

"We'll take you to a hospital. They'll check you over and tell you that you're not sick."

"I'm not waiting all night," Zoe called out.

"Going to the hospital is what killed Evelyn. I have to go. I'll call you when I can. It might not be for a few days. Maybe longer. Stay away from that plant. Better yet, don't go outside."

"Come home, Piper. If you come home now we'll sit down and talk and help you figure out what is going on."

She momentarily closed her eyes, wishing she could make her mum understand. "If I-" She broke off, unable to say 'die'. "Someone else might call you if the worst happens." She disconnected the call in the middle of her mum's pleas for her to come home, turning off the communication device. It took a moment before she could bring herself to get in the vehicle. This time she sat by the window, Selene having moved over for her.

Selene squeezed her hand tight as Zoe pulled out onto the road. "I don't care what she says." She nodded towards Zoe. "We're going to make it."

Piper couldn't answer, not without bursting into tears. And she refused to do that in front of Zoe. She could imagine the comments that would cause. Nodding, she leaned her head back and closed her eyes. What did it feel like when Dawn was growing in your lungs? She remembered the dissected lungs on the bench in the laboratory and forced the image from her mind. No way. That wasn't happening to her. Other images invaded her mind. Dandelion like fluff floating around her.

Selene started coughing, drawing her hand away to cover her mouth, even though it was already covered by the medical mask. When she finished, her breathing sounded laboured.

"You better not be coughing up blood," Zoe said. "If you are, you can get out of my vehicle."

Piper stared at the mask. It remained white. She saw Selene's questioning gaze in the early morning light that was starting to fill the sky. She shook her head. There was no blood. She held Selene's gaze a moment longer, seeing the flash of relief before worry crowded in again. She took hold of Selene's hand, unable to ask Zoe what blood meant.

It was Wyatt who asked the question. "What does it mean if you cough up blood?"

"That you're highly contagious and will probably drown in your own blood in less than a day."

"Zoe." There was a warning in Gibson's voice.

"What? Did you want me to lie to them?"

"No, but you could have explained it better."

"Life is cruel. If they don't realise that already, then it's time they did," Zoe stated.

Piper's lungs felt like they tightened. No. She wasn't about to drown in her own blood. Could she take the drugs before she showed symptoms? Was there a test to find out if she was infected? How much longer was it going to take to reach Kyndall's lab? She had so many questions to ask Emerson.

Chapter Sixteen

When they arrived at the compound, Piper didn't have the chance to ask Emerson a single question. He rushed each of them off to a separate quarantine room, saying he didn't have time to talk. There was work to be done.

Alone, she dragged the mask off and tossed it on the floor before she tried the door of the quarantine room. It was locked. Looking around she soon found there was no way out. The room contained a single bed, a small table, one chair and a door leading into a narrow bathroom. Everything was stainless steel except for the mattress, which was plastic coated. There wasn't even a sheet on the bed. Not knowing what else to do, and completely exhausted, Piper lay on the bed to wait. She fell asleep, waking to find Gibson sitting beside her, wearing his protective gear.

She struggled to sit up, fear making her heart race. "You think I'm infected?"

He shook his head. "Zoe and Emerson are being cautious."

"How will we know?" She needed to know now. She couldn't stand to wait.

"In two days Emerson can take a scan of your lungs and see if there's any growth. If there's none after a week, you're clear."

"I have to stay in here for a week?" She'd be climbing the walls before a couple of days were over.

He shrugged. "I tried to tell them four days is enough." He shrugged again. "Zoe isn't easy to convince."

"What do I do in here for a week?" There was no way she was staying that long. She had to find a way to convince them to let her out earlier. She couldn't be infected. But what if she was? She had no idea what to think.

He held up a communication device. "I've downloaded the research details onto this."

"Where's mine?"

"You can't use it. Someone might track you with it."

She reluctantly took the device. "Who owns this one?"

"No one. It's a spare."

She put it beside her on the bed. "How are Selene and Wyatt?"

"The same."

"Are you treating them?"

"Yeah." He held up a hand when she started to ask more questions. "I'll tell you the moment there's any change. Good or bad."

"Okay."

"Do you need anything?"

She glanced towards the door. "A key? Or a code."

Gibson chuckled, reaching for her hand. "You're going to be okay."

She looked at her hand in his, the protective white glove covering his hand. She wanted to believe him. Desperately wanted to. She met his gaze. "And what if I'm not?"

"You will be." His hand tightened on hers.

She looked away from the intensity of his gaze. "Will you stay with me for a while?" She didn't want to be alone. Her thoughts were likely to return to the dissected lungs filled with fine white hairs. And the dandelion like fluff floating gently on the air.

"Sure. What did you want to do?"

Escape. She sighed, knowing he wouldn't grant that wish. "It was meant to be the discovery of a lifetime." Her words were soft, escaping before she could prevent them.

"It is."

Her gaze was drawn to his. "How can you say that? Dawn is a killer."

"A discovery of a lifetime is neither good nor bad. It's a major discovery. And Dawn is certainly that for all that she's also a killer."

She thought over his words for a moment, slowly nodding. "Maybe, but I'd expected a good discovery."

A sad smile formed and his hand momentarily tightened on hers again. "So did we all."

She felt guilty for causing that look. The one she now knew meant he was thinking of his father. She tried to think of a way to distract him. She was out of ideas. "Do you want to go over the research with me?" She nodded towards the communication device. If she couldn't distract him, maybe she could distract herself. She didn't want to die.

"Sounds good."

She was surprised the laugh his words startled from her sounded normal. "You really need to get out more if you think that's something good to do."

"That sounds like a better idea. Where shall we go once we finish dealing with Dawn?"

She met his gaze again. "Are you asking me out on a date?"

"Yep. Not the first time if you remember."

Her lips slowly curved into a smile as she tried not to think of death, lungs filled with white threads and dandelion like fluff. "Now that does sound like a good idea. How about a movie?"

"It's a date." He picked up the communication device, continuing to hold her hand. "Do you want to start at the beginning?"

Her smile faded as the images she'd barely kept away flooded back in. She refused to let them overwhelm her. "That's probably the most logical place." She kept her voice light even though she felt like screaming that none of this was fair.

Gibson stayed with her for several hours, reading the research and talking it over with her. Eventually Zoe sent him a message on his communication device telling him to stop slacking off and come help.

Before he left, Gibson paused at the doorway to stare at Piper who continued to sit on the bed. "If you need me, I'm listed in the contacts." He gestured towards the communication device she held. "But don't call anyone else. We don't want to be tracked down."

"Okay." She continued to stare through the glass

panel of the door long after he'd left, having paused in the short corridor outside her door to be sprayed by jets that would freeze any spores that might be on him. She didn't want to die. Her lungs burned and she tried to convince herself it was from trying not to cry. Once she started there was a good chance she wouldn't stop and there was research to do. Emerson and Jerome had to have done something different. She needed to figure it out in a hurry. It was a good thing she'd always enjoyed science.

It took awhile before she could bring herself to return to reading the research notes. They were full of data and facts, nothing standing out. The doses had been calculated on body weight. All of them had been given at the same time. By the end of the day, she was almost relieved to eat the meal Zoe had delivered and fall asleep.

Sleeping didn't help. It was broken and filled with bits of random data, dandelion like fluff and dissected lungs. Several times she woke, sitting up as her heart raced and her breathing sounded like she'd been running. By five a.m. she gave up trying to sleep and had been awake for a while, restlessly prowling the area, when Gibson visited her.

He stood by the door, wearing his protective gear. "How do you feel?"

"Bored." Angry, scared, not wanting to die.

He smiled fleetingly. "Do you feel okay?"

"I wouldn't have a clue. Every symptom I read, I half expect to have. So I wouldn't know whether I was suffering any symptoms or if it's in my imagination from reading about it so much." She dropped onto the bed, clasping her hands together.

Gibson crossed the room to sit beside her, untangling her hands and taking hold of one of them. "You don't feel well?"

She shrugged. "I don't know. I'm tired, worried about everyone and," she met his gaze and held it a moment before she continued, "absolutely terrified." She glanced away before meeting his gaze again. "This was meant to be a good thing. When I first read about Dawn, I was so excited. Now…" She shrugged again.

"We all were. My father would tell us every single thing about his day. We listened avidly for a while, but eventually lost our excitement. There's only so many times you can hear about the same experiment."

She smiled weakly, thinking about her parents who'd probably been bored with her ramblings about Dawn.

"He stopped telling us things and at first we were

relieved. Then we started to worry about what was wrong." Gibson fell silent, his eyes unfocused.

"How'd you find out what was going on?"

It was nearly a minute before he spoke. "They fell sick. He told us then. He called and told us not to come out to his lab. It wasn't as big as this back then. It was simpler." Again Gibson fell silent. His fingers tightened on hers. "We didn't see him until nearly the end. Macie called. She told us we needed to see him before it was too late. That was when we discovered what he'd done here. All the changes he'd made to protect us. It's amazing how quickly things can be built when you've got money."

"I'm sorry." The words seemed inadequate.

"We weren't with him at the end. Emerson had wandered off. It was pouring rain and he was delirious. We had to find him. We were worried he'd spread the infection. Jerome helped. We tried to tell him he was too sick, but he insisted, wearing a medical mask to prevent the spread of the spores. We were out there all night. When we found Emerson, we realised we'd lost Jerome. It took hours to find him. He'd collapsed and neither of us had noticed. When we got back to the lab, we found Dad had passed away. Alone."

"I'm sorry." She wished there was something she

could say to him, but no words came to mind. What could she say? Nothing that could change what had happened.

The door opened and Emerson stood there, wearing protective gear. "I think we can do blood tests to find out if someone is infected."

Piper rose to her feet, Gibson standing with her, continuing to hold her hand. "I want one."

Emerson nodded, coming further into the room and holding up his hand to show the needle he held. "I can't guarantee it. Still figuring it out. The other two show signs of Dawn's DNA in their bloodstream."

"I don't care. If it'll get me out of this room earlier, you can do all the blood tests you want." She desperately needed to know if she'd die. The waiting was worse than the knowing.

Emerson gestured towards the chair. "I've been focusing on diagnosing the infection, but it doesn't show up like that. It might seem like an infection, but in reality, Dawn takes over the host. Last night we had the first two lab rats from an infected batch survive. They show signs of improvement, but have damaged lungs. I don't know if I can heal their lungs and I don't have the time to figure it out. Not with everyone that needs testing regularly. Even if your friends survive, their lungs might be like that of the rats. Barely able to work." He fell silent as he took a sample of blood from Piper. "I'm going to test this right away then infect another batch of rats. I'll take hourly blood samples to see how soon they can be diagnosed that way."

Chapter Seventeen

Piper watched Emerson leave the room, desperately hoping this would work. She didn't know how much longer she could manage to stay in the quarantine room. Or how long she could wait to find out if she'd survive.

"Call us if you need something." Gibson paused at the door. "Do you need anything before I go?"

"Breakfast."

Gibson nodded. "I'll let Zoe know. She's on kitchen duty this week."

Piper wondered if she should be rethinking eating today. She'd survived last night's meal, but that didn't mean much with how volatile Zoe was. Zoe didn't like her. Actually, she didn't seem to like anyone and went out of her way to make sure everyone disliked her. "Okay." She supposed she had to eat. She certainly didn't want to get sick.

The rest of the day Piper alternated between reading the research and pacing the small room. Zoe brought her breakfast and lunch. She didn't see anyone else. It was almost ten p.m. and she was considering calling Gibson, and asking him if someone was going to bring her dinner, when the door opened. Piper rose from the bed she'd been lying on. "I was starting to wonder where everyone was."

Wearing protective clothing, Gibson came into the room. "Emerson will be here in a minute to take another sample of blood. If it comes up clear, you can leave quarantine."

"He's finished testing the rats?"

Gibson nodded. "Most of them showed signs of Dawn DNA within six hours. One took nearly eleven hours."

Piper didn't know how to feel. Before she had the chance to decide, Emerson entered and her stomach lurched, making her feel sick. She sat on the bed and tried to remain positive. All she could think about was how the room had been filled with the spores. The dandelion like fluff had been everywhere. 'Wish on a dandelion.' The words popped into her head, accompanied by an image of her mum holding out one gone to seed, a smile on her face as she bent down for Piper to take it. How many years ago had that been? She doubted she'd been old enough to attend school. How she wished Dawn had never been discovered. She closed her eyes when Emerson drew blood. Not opening them again until Emerson had left without a word.

She stared at the closed door. "How long will it take him to check?"

Zoe burst through the door before Gibson had a chance to answer. She was wearing her protective gear. "It's out."

"What's out?" Piper asked at the same time as Gibson said, "I hope you're not expecting us to know what you're talking about."

Zoe remained just inside the door. "Dawn. The backers have told everyone. It's on all the news channels. The world is going crazy. Half of them think it's a hoax, the other half are talking the end of the world."

Gibson took a step towards his sister then halted, looking back at Piper.

She forced herself to speak the words he was obviously hoping for. "I don't mind if you go and see. Make sure you come back and let me out if Emerson says I'm clear."

Gibson stared at her a moment longer before he

shook his head. "I'll wait with you. Emerson shouldn't be too long."

"They're burning them," Zoe said.

"Why isn't anyone telling them?" Gibson asked.

Piper looked from one to the other. "What does that mean?"

Zoe gave her a look as if to tell her she was an idiot. "Fire spreads it. Only freezing will kill the plant."

Piper's mind was momentarily blank. "My parents. What about my parents?"

"We'll bring them here," Gibson said.

"Oh no we won't. You can't save the world. We've got to think of ourselves first," Zoe said.

"This place can support fifty adults," Gibson said.

"Yeah, exactly. That's not many people. We don't have space for dead weight. We need to find people who are useful," Zoe said.

"My parents are not dead weight." Piper glared at Zoe. A message came through on Gibson's communication device. After reading it he turned to Piper, removing his breathing mask to reveal a grin.

"I'm clear?" She took half a step towards him. "That was Emerson?"

Gibson crossed the distance between them, wrapping his arms around her. "You're clear."

She tightened her arms around him, laughing.

Relief swamped her before it was replaced by fear for Selene and her parents. "I need to save my parents."

"It might already be too late. They could be contaminated." Zoe left the room before either of them could speak.

Piper wanted to argue with her. Wanted to chase after her and demand that she take the words back. "Can I see Selene?"

Gibson nodded "You can't go in there. But you can talk to her from outside the room."

"She's alone?" She thought of how he'd talked about his father dying alone. She didn't want that for Selene. Actually, she didn't want death for Selene. Nor did she want her friend to be alone during any of the waiting.

Gibson shook his head. "Wyatt is with her. They both wanted it that way."

"I want to see her."

Gibson let her go, linking his fingers through hers as he nodded. He led her through several corridors coming to a stop at a door with a large glass window in it. "They can hear you." He pointed to a speaker in the ceiling.

"Selene?" She stepped close to the door, pressing her hand against the glass. "Selene?"

Selene struggled to sit up on the bed, Wyatt on

a plastic coated mattress on the floor. Selene looked at him first before looking towards the door. "You're okay?"

Piper nodded. "And you will be too." Her throat tightened and she tried to force herself to smile. How had Selene grown paler? She hadn't thought it possible. "We're working on figuring it out."

"I don't think you've got much time. It's getting harder to breathe." Selene looked towards Wyatt who hadn't moved. "Wyatt?" Selene struggled to her feet, moving to Wyatt's side where she collapsed beside him. She landed half on the floor, half on the mattress, shaking his shoulder. "Wyatt. Don't you dare desert me. You said you wouldn't leave me in here alone."

Piper couldn't take her gaze off Selene and Wyatt even though she wanted to look away. Didn't want to watch her friend or listen to the panic in her voice.

"Wyatt!" Selene shook him hard, doubling over with a coughing fit.

Wyatt opened his eyes and tried to smile, only managing to grimace. "I'm here." He struggled to sit up, but began coughing. He rolled to his side and when he finished coughing, his hands were flecked with red.

Gibson swore.

Piper turned to face him, about to ask him if Zoe

had told the truth. She stopped. Selene and Wyatt would hear. Not that she needed to ask once she'd seen his expression. Zoe had spoken the truth. She faced the window again. "Can I get either of you anything?"

Selene smiled weakly. "A new pair of lungs?"

Piper tried to smile like her friend expected. It didn't last long. "I'll see what I can do." She hurried away, Gibson following her.

When they stepped through the door that separated the corridor, Gibson dragged Piper close, holding her tight. "I'm sorry."

She could hear it in his voice. He believed they were already dead. "We have to do something. We need to figure this out." She pulled back to meet his gaze. "I can't lose her. I can't." Pain arrowed through her, making it hard to breathe. Images of the white threads came to mind. "We have to save her." The words came out a whisper. "Please, Gib."

He dragged her close again. "I'm so sorry."

Chapter Eighteen

Piper remained pressed against Gibson, shaking her head. "Don't give up. There must be something different about what you did for Emerson and Jerome."

"They had the same drugs as the others. We didn't give them anything else when they ended up with fevers after being outside in the rain. We used cool baths to bring their temperatures down in case any medication we gave them might interfere with the drugs they were on. I'm sorry, Piper. We've gone over the facts so many times."

The words fever and cool baths rang in her mind. "Did anyone else have a fever?"

Gibson drew back to look at her, slowly shaking his head. "That's not a symptom Dawn gives you. It only affects your lungs. Eats away at them."

"They're the only ones who survived. That's the only difference. A fever and cool baths."

"Fire spreads Dawn. It can't be the fever."

"What about the cool baths?"

"They weren't that cool. Nowhere near cold enough to have killed Dawn or slowed it."

"It's the only difference. It has to mean something." She tried not to wince at the desperation she heard in her voice. "Gib, we have to try something." The desperation remained, clawing at her insides, colouring her words.

"I'll talk to Emerson and Zoe. Did you want to come with me?"

She started to say yes, then worried Zoe might disagree to try using fever as a means of killing Dawn. "I'll see what Selene and Wyatt think." She held onto Gibson a moment longer before drawing away from him, taking several steps backwards before she turned and ran to Selene. She pressed her hand against the glass window, words fleeing when she saw her friend curled up beside Wyatt. They were dying, already looked dead. Their unnaturally pale skin made them look like corpses. If they were going to do something they had to do it in a hurry.

Selene opened her eyes. There was a moment of

confusion in them. It cleared and she smiled at Piper. "Did you figure it out?"

She swallowed, the lump in her throat making it difficult. "I'm not sure." She paused a moment, taking a deep breath before she told Selene her idea.

Wyatt opened his eyes. "Do it. Raise my temperature."

Footsteps behind Piper had her spinning to face that direction. It was Emerson, dressed in protective clothing and wearing a breathing mask. "They want to try."

Emerson walked past her. "Raising your temperature to excessive levels could cause other problems."

"I don't care," Selene said. "If we don't do something, we're dead anyway." She clutched Wyatt's hand.

"Proteins and body fats will be exposed to temperature stressors, which can threaten their integrity," Emerson said.

"What does that mean?" Wyatt's words were broken by laboured breathing.

"Cellular stress, necrosis and seizures are a possibility."

Wyatt slowly shook his head. "Say it in English."

Selene demanded, "What is necrosis?"

"The death of most cells in an organ. Sometimes the death of all of them." Silence hung in the air at Emerson's words. "It could kill you. Is that clear enough?"

"But it might not," Selene said. "It might kill Dawn."

"Even if you survive, you might end up with brain damage," Emerson said.

Piper pressed her fingers against her mouth to keep back the protests she wanted to make. Her idea was sounding worse by the second. But it was Selene and Wyatt's choice. They were the ones dying.

Selene turned to Wyatt, neither of them speaking. After a moment Selene smiled, reaching out to lightly touch his cheek before facing the door. "We want to try. Your drugs aren't working."

"They work, just not as fast as Dawn spreads," Gibson said. "It kills it off, but not quickly enough."

"A high fever might be what is needed to slow Dawn down long enough for the drugs to work," Zoe said.

Piper turned to her in surprise, not having noticed her join them.

Zoe turned to Gibson. "The world is going crazy. There's riots, shootings, looting and a massive amount of people trying to access our old website.

Something has changed and I can access it again too. Do you want me to upload all the details again?"

Gibson looked from Piper to Zoe. "I-" He broke off, looking between them again.

Emerson made a shooing motion. "I have this. Don't bother putting up the evidence. Keep it simple. Most will be in a panic. Explain step by step what they should do, where they can get supplies and how to avoid contamination. Tell the ones who aren't infected to live in the Snowy Mountains. A pity our country doesn't have more colder areas than it does."

Gibson turned to Piper.

She nodded. "Let everyone know what they should be doing. You said they shouldn't be burning Dawn. Tell them. We need to destroy her. Tell them how to do that." If more people knew, maybe they had a chance.

With a nod, Gibson strode after Zoe.

Piper faced Emerson. "What can I do to help?"

"Not a lot. I'll turn up the temperature and gather warm clothes to get things started. Then I need to look through my supplies to see what I have that will raise their temperatures." Emerson hurried away.

Piper felt useless as she stared after him.

"Piper?"

She turned to look at Selene. "Yeah?"

"We need to tell our families what is going on. Your parents, my grandparents, my aunt. We have people we can save." Selene looked at Wyatt. "Do you have anyone else?"

He shook his head. "They're dead. I'm the last one left."

Piper was momentarily lost for words. "I'll call them. I'll ask Gibson to give my device back to me." She took a step away, not wanting to leave Selene.

"Go." Selene smiled wryly. "It's not like I'm going anywhere. I'll be here when you get back. Save our families, Piper. I don't want to lose anyone else." Selene brushed moisture from her eyes.

Piper took another step away. She didn't want to lose anyone either. "Okay. I'll convince Gibson to let them come here." She strode away, having no idea where to find him. Entering the laboratory it occurred to her she could call and ask him where he was and how to get to his location.

Gibson answered immediately. "Is everything okay?"

"Where are you? I need to talk to you."

"I'm at Zoe's place."

"Oh." This wasn't a conversation she could have while Zoe argued that no one was allowed in the compound.

"I'll meet you outside. Will that do?"

Relief rushed through her. "Yes." Disconnecting the call, she hurried outside and ran into Gibson.

His arms went around her. "I'd love to think your rush was due to your desperation to be with me."

A smile reluctantly appeared, staying longer than Piper would have expected with the problems looming ahead of them. "I need to save my family. And Selene's family. Or at least what's left of it."

"It could be too late."

"We might have discovered a way to save them." She drew back from him. "I have to try. If you'd had the chance to save your father, wouldn't you have tried?"

"We did try. And nothing helped."

She heard the pain in his voice, taking his hand to hold on tightly. "Then don't let me suffer what you're suffering. Help me save my family."

"They'll have to go in quarantine."

"I don't mind. And I'm sure they won't either."

Gibson smiled fleetingly. "Zoe is going to be angry."

She stepped closer. "I'll protect you from her."

He chuckled, taking hold of her other hand. "It's you I'm worried about. Me she'll eventually forgive. She always does."

"How do you put up with how angry she is?"

Sorrow filled his eyes. "She wasn't always angry. She used to be the easygoing one."

"Oh."

A half smile formed, vanishing before it could become a full one. "Like she said, life can be cruel." He paused a moment. "One day she might be able to smile again. But for now, she's terrified none of us will survive and doesn't want to get close to anyone else and go through the heartbreak of losing them."

"Aren't you terrified?" She knew she was.

He grinned. "I'm not that crazy. Of course I'm terrified." His grin faded. "But that gives me a reason to enjoy every second. I don't know how many more of them there'll be."

Zoe strode towards them. "I thought you were going to help. We've been flooded with people asking questions. At this rate the server is likely to crash."

Gibson held out his hand. "I need Piper's device."

Zoe backed away from him, shaking her head. "No. You're not bringing anyone else here."

Gibson followed her. "Zoe."

"Are you trying to get us killed?"

He kept his hand out. "Dad wouldn't want you to

turn your back on anyone. He would have given his meal to a starving person and gone hungry himself."

"And where did that get him?" Zoe demanded. "Dead. Not here with us." She drew the communication device out of a pocket and slammed it against his palm. "Here. Get us killed." She pointed to the mesh above. "Do you think that will work forever? One day we'll have to move. Something is sure to fail and it'll no longer freeze the spores. How will we move if we have dozens we need to take with us? Start learning how to travel light." Zoe stalked back to her cottage before Gibson could speak.

Chapter Nineteen

Piper joined Gibson, slipping her hand in his. "Will it work?" She glanced upwards.

"It'll work. It was tested on a smaller scale. It can also be electrified. So can the outer fence. Someone needs to go out there and trim everything back before much longer. We no longer need to hide that we're here. It's more important that the fence line is clear now."

She hoped he wasn't trying to reassure her. His words caused her heart to race. It sounded like he was preparing for battle. She couldn't focus on that now. There were people she had to collect. "Can we pick up my family?"

"They'll have to meet us somewhere. We can't go into the city. It's too dangerous. And we can't give them our location. We don't know who might be listening."

"Okay. What do I tell them?"

Gibson held out her communication device. "Convince them to listen to me. I'll let them know where to go."

It took her a few seconds to be able to bring herself to take the device. She didn't know if she was ready for this. What if her parents didn't answer? What if she'd left it too late? She turned on the device, her stomach twisting and rolling as she waited. It felt like it took longer than usual, but she knew that was only because she dreaded what might have happened. They had to be okay. It wasn't like they went out much and as far as she knew, no one in their apartment building had a plant.

The call was answered immediately. "Piper."

For a moment she couldn't speak at the relief she heard in her mum's voice. It echoed her own.

"Piper?" Worry replaced the relief that had initially been in Tricia's voice. "Is that you, Piper?"

"Yeah." She cleared her throat. "I'm okay, Mum."

"We were so worried."

"What about you and Dad?"

"We went with Linda to collect her parents and came back here. It's crazy out there. Are you safe, where you are?"

"Yeah. I'm outside the city."

"Stay there. Don't come home. If you're safe, don't leave."

She tried to swallow past the lump in her throat. "Mum-" Her voice broke and she started again. "Mum, there's someone I need you to talk to. We're going to get all of you out of the city."

"No, I won't have you risk yourself to-"

Piper interrupted. "His name is Gib. Here he is."

"Piper-"

Ignoring her mum, she handed the communication device to Gibson. "Don't let her talk you out of getting them out of the city."

He nodded before speaking to Tricia. "You can stop worrying. I'm not about to put Piper in danger. I'll give you a location to go to. I'll call you when you reach there so I can give you further details." He listened for a moment before reassuring Tricia that everything would be okay.

Piper wished she'd put the communication device on speaker mode so she could have heard what her mum was saying. Before she could ask Gibson to change the mode, he was saying goodbye and handing the device back.

"We need to get ready. From now on we always wear protective gear when we're outside the compound. Who knows how far Dawn has spread with all the burnings."

Piper nodded, not wanting to risk her lungs being filled with white threads. She tried not to think about Selene and Wyatt's lungs. How bad were they? "I'll let Selene know her grandparents and aunt are safe. I won't be long."

"Okay. I'll see you back out here shortly."

She returned to the corridor, staring through the glass pane at Selene and Wyatt sprawled on the mattress. Their skin remained unnaturally pale, but there was a flush across their cheeks that hadn't been there earlier. Was that a good thing? She didn't know, but hoped it was.

As if feeling Piper watching her, Selene opened her eyes. For a moment she stared at Piper as if she didn't know her. "Piper? Did you talk to Aunt Linda?"

Piper pressed her hand against the glass. It felt warm. "Her and your grandparents are with my parents."

"They're safe?"

"Yes."

Selene struggled to sit up. "Don't tell them about me. Not yet. Let them get to safety first."

"But-"

"Please. They must be so scared. My grandparents

more than Aunt Linda. They've already lost my mum and Zoe will make them go into quarantine. Let them get over all of that first. Please, Piper."

Piper wanted to argue, but Selene didn't look like she could cope with an argument. "Okay." She glanced at Wyatt. "How are you both doing?"

Selene dropped back onto the mattress. "All I want to do is sleep. And I'm hot. Too hot. Emerson gave us personal temperature monitors." Selene lifted her hand so Piper could see the metal band around her wrist. "We have to cool ourselves down if our temperatures are too high."

"You're going to get well," Piper stated. She couldn't lose Selene. "I have to go." She turned away before Selene could see the tears in her eyes. Somehow they'd beat Dawn and destroy every single plant. She ran through the building. This discovery was a worse disaster than the Mars colonisation project. Stepping outside, Piper ran into Gibson for the second time that night, unable to clearly see him through the blur of tears. "Sorry."

"Is Selene-" Gibson broke off, his arms going around her. "Is-"

She shook her head. "No. She's the same. Well, other than hot. But I can't lose her. We've been best friends forever. I know she's not perfect and we fight at times, but we always make up and we're always there for each other."

"We'll do everything we can to keep Selene and Wyatt alive. If we can save them, we'll be able to save other people."

She drew back, wiping at her eyes with the back of her hand. "This means a lot to you."

"It was my father's work. In the end, that was all he wanted to do. Discover a way to survive Dawn. Not for himself, but for us." He gestured towards the vehicle. "Your gear is on the passenger seat. As soon as you have it on, we can go."

She dressed in record time, sitting in the front passenger seat next to Gibson. "Thank you for doing this."

"As I said, it was my father's work. If he'd only wanted to save Zoe and me, he wouldn't have made the compound so large."

"Zoe doesn't agree?"

Gibson glanced at her. "She does, but she doesn't trust anyone. She also refuses to care about anyone and go through the pain of losing them again."

Piper had no idea what to say so she remained silent, staring out the window. It was quiet on the outskirts of the city, but she could see a glow in the sky, a red hue to it that normally wasn't there. How many fires were burning across the city?

Gibson pulled up at a lookout, sitting in the dark for a moment before he spoke. "Call your parents." He got out of the vehicle, taking Vision Enhancers with him.

Piper followed, calling her parents and putting the communication device on speaker mode. She avoided video since she didn't want to scare her parents with the gear she wore. They'd see it soon enough.

Tricia answered instantly. "I didn't think it'd take so long for you to call. Is everything okay?"

Gibson spoke before Piper could. "If you're in position, turn your vehicle lights off and on four times." He looked through the Vision Enhancers.

Piper wished there was a second pair so she could see her parents.

"I want you to drive out of the parking area and take a left," Gibson said.

"You can see us from wherever you are?" Alistair asked.

"Yes. Now drive along there until I tell you to turn off." Gibson continued to look through the Vision Enhancers.

"Would we be able to see you?" Tricia asked.

"Without VEs I can't see you," Piper said.

"You have military equipment?" There was fear in Linda's voice.

Until she'd spoken, Piper had forgotten Selene's family were in the vehicle too. Hearing her parents' voices had pushed all other concerns from her mind. Should she say something about Selene? Why hadn't they asked anything? Did they fear what answer they'd receive?

"Take the next right and the next left after that," Gibson said.

"Do we have far to go?" Alistair asked.

"Not much–" Gibson broke off at the sound of a vehicle headed towards the lookout, turning in that direction.

Piper faced the sound too, watching the lights come closer. She muted their end of the call, ignoring her mum's demand to know what was going on. "What should we do?"

"Give me your device and get in the vehicle."

She shook her head. "What about my parents?"

He took the communication device from her. "I'll sort it out. Go on. Open a window so you can hear what's going on. I want you to drive off if I say the word boot."

"I can't leave you behind."

"Hurry. They've nearly reached us and I need to

sort your parents out." He turned away, looking through the Vision Enhancers again and turning mute off. "You've gone too far. Go back and turn down the first right. After about ten kilometres take a left and travel along there until you come across the first left. Pull up and wait until you hear from us."

Chapter Twenty

Piper got in the vehicle, sitting in the driver's seat in case Gibson said the word 'boot'. She listened to him reassure her parents and Selene's family, hanging up when the other vehicle came to a stop. She twisted in the seat so she could see them, shielding her eyes from the spotlights.

Gibson tossed her communication device in the window to her as he walked past. "There's no need to get out of your vehicle. There's nothing up here."

A door opened and a man got out of the front passenger seat. "Then why are you up here and where did you get that outfit from?"

Piper's heart sank at the size of the man. He had to be a fair bit taller than Gibson and easily twice as broad, all of it muscle. Why wasn't Gibson getting in the vehicle so they could get out of here?

"Came to see what was happening in the city."

Gibson stood by the back door of his vehicle, resting a hand on the roof. "Doesn't look too good down there."

A man got out of the driver's seat, leaning against the door of his vehicle. "I want your outfit. No one else has anything like that. Or at least not that I've seen."

"A fine filter dust mask or a medical mask will do a similar job," Gibson said. "This gear is too small for you."

Piper wanted to yell at him to stop talking and get in so she could drive away from the two men who were a similar size. What was Gibson waiting for? To be attacked?

The driver stepped away from his vehicle and took a couple of steps towards Gibson. "I'm not going to ask again. I want your outfit. Either give it to me or I'll take it."

"I'm not about to let you take it." Gibson opened the backdoor, keeping his gaze on the men. He took a metal bar off the back seat. "You can try if you want."

The men shared a look, both striding towards Gibson.

Piper nearly demanded to know what Gibson was thinking.

"Good thing I didn't leave this in the boot," Gibson said.

It took a second for the word to sink in. He'd finally spoken the word she'd been waiting for. Turning in the seat, she started the vehicle and was about to look over her shoulder when the back door slammed shut.

"Drive!" Gibson ordered from where he sat on the back seat.

She turned the steering wheel, accelerating as the men reached the vehicle. One of them hit the vehicle as she drove past, both of them cursing and threatening them. "Why did you wait so long?" She headed down the steep road.

"Be careful. The automatic override has been disabled. You'll be able to go above the speed limit."

Her grip tightened on the steering wheel. "Why would you do that?"

"For times like this. They'll have no chance of catching up with us."

"Why did you stay outside talking to them?"

"To give us a few extra seconds head start. Now they have to get back in their vehicle before they can follow."

Piper checked the mirror when bright light filled

their vehicle. "Looks like it didn't slow them down too much."

"It only had to be enough for us to leave them behind and lose them on the back roads to the city." Gibson leaned forward. "Take the first left when you reach the bottom of the hill."

"We can't go into the city. There are fires out of control everywhere." Surely he'd noticed that while they'd been at the lookout. Reaching the bottom of the hill, she slowed for the corner, but it wasn't enough. Her breath caught in her throat as she struggled to stay on the road, unaccustomed to having full control over a vehicle.

"We're not going into the city, only the outskirts. You need to remember the vehicle isn't going to brake for you if you're going too fast."

Her jaw tightened. Like she hadn't already realised that. "I'm surprised my parents haven't rung."

"I put a temporary block on incoming calls. They'll be able to get through again in a few minutes."

Anger rushed through her. "They must be terrified. Why would you do that? It's not your device."

"I didn't want the men to be distracted by anything." Gibson paused a moment. "Take a right up here. This road has a lot of corners. As soon as you can't see them, pull into one of the driveways and turn off the lights."

She glanced in the mirror, the lights from the vehicle behind remained bright, the distance between them having grown. Slowing, she took the next corner fast, her grip on the wheel tightening as she tried to slow a little more. "A vehicle chase wasn't what I expected. I don't normally drive much." Nor had she been driving for long.

"You're doing okay."

It didn't feel like it. She kept thinking they were going to come off the road. The lights vanished. "Now?"

"Give it a couple more corners," Gibson said.

The lights filled their vehicle again and she took the next curve in the road, slowing when it felt like they'd roll. "If we ever manage to pull over, you can drive." Her communication device signalled an incoming call.

"Want me to get that?"

She couldn't bring herself to glance down and see if it was her parents, but she doubted it'd be anyone else. "They can wait." There was no way she'd be able to concentrate on her driving and reassure her parents at the same time. Light filled the vehicle again and she took another corner, the light disappearing only seconds after it had appeared.

"Okay. Pull over into the first driveway after the next corner," Gibson said.

"What if someone comes out to see what's going on?" Piper was relieved her communication device fell silent.

"I don't think many people are going to be wanting to step outside their homes. Especially not in this area. They'll be barricaded inside and hoping this mess goes away before it reaches them out here."

Piper held her breath as she took the next corner, trying to slow the vehicle as she searched for a suitable driveway. She slowed further, not wanting to roll the vehicle when they were close to escaping their pursuers. Spotting a driveway with a less sharp entrance, she slowed further, pulled onto it and continued towards the shadowy buildings she could see at the end.

"Turn your lights off and park near those shrubs." Gibson pointed to the location.

She did as he said, turning in her seat to watch the road behind them the moment she was parked. Bright lights continued past. "Was that them?"

"It looked like it." Gibson opened the door. "Ready to get in the passenger seat?"

She was past ready. Picking up her communication device, she got out and walked around the vehicle and clambered in the other side, collapsing on the seat. She needed to call her parents, but that would have to wait a few minutes. Her heart raced and she felt shaky. Dropping her communication device onto her lap, she clasped her hands together. It didn't help.

"Are you going to call your parents?"

"Yeah." It took her a few more seconds before she could bring herself to call, putting the device on speaker and cancelling the video feed when her parents requested it.

"Is everything okay?" Tricia's voice was filled with fear, her words hushed.

Piper frowned. "What's wrong?"

"Where do you need us to go next?" Linda demanded. Her voice was also kept low.

"What is going on?" Piper tried to keep the fear from her voice. Why hadn't she answered their earlier call?

"Fires are headed this way and people are escaping by any means necessary."

Piper closed her eyes when Selene's grandfather spoke, hearing her mum trying to hush him. "What happened?"

"People were shot," Linda said.

"Not us," Tricia hurriedly reassured her.

Piper turned to Gibson. "Tell them where to go. They can't stay where they are."

Gibson started the vehicle, reversing down the driveway, turning on the lights. "Can you remain there another ten minutes? We aren't far away."

"You're not bringing Piper here," Alistair said. "Give us an address."

"I can't do that." Gibson pulled out onto the road, heading back in the direction they'd come from.

Why not?" Linda demanded.

"Because conversations on devices can be listened in on and I don't want everyone having our location," Gibson said.

Piper heard Selene's grandmother in the background, saying they were going to die. "Tell them something. Give them a location," she urged Gibson. "We can't leave them where they are for ten minutes." She had visions of mobs running around her family, fires racing towards them.

"You're not bringing Piper here," Alistair stated.

"There's no other way to collect you," Gibson said.

Piper started to tell her dad that she was fine. There was no reason why Gibson couldn't bring her to them.

"What are you doing?" Linda demanded. "Stop the vehicle."

"We won't be here," Alistair said. "Take Piper back to safety."

"No." Piper requested video feed, but no one accepted. "Dad-"

Gibson interrupted her. "We're going there anyway. If you're not there it'll be a wasted trip."

"Let me out of the vehicle. I'll wait for them alone if you don't want to stop," Linda demanded.

"Dad-" This time Piper was interrupted by the call ending. She tried calling, but no one answered. "Can't you go faster?" She turned to Gibson. "Please?" She nearly grabbed his arm, but drew back her hand, worried she'd cause him to have an accident.

"Once we're on the next road. This one twists and turns too much."

Chapter Twenty-One

Piper clasped her hands together, trying not to think of everything that could go wrong. There were hundreds of things and it felt like every single scenario played through her mind in graphic detail. An endless loop of horror. "This was meant to be something special. Not just the discovery of a lifetime." She couldn't stop thinking that. It felt like it was on her mind every minute of the day.

"Somehow we'll recover from it."

"How do you know?" She tried to see Gibson's expression, but the glow from the interior wasn't bright enough to clearly tell what he was feeling. Nor was much of his face visible past his protective gear. "No one can say that."

"Maybe not us specifically, but the human race. It will recover."

"You don't have to make up comments to try and make me feel better."

Gibson laughed softly. "I truly believe it even if you don't. Look at history. At what we've faced as a race and the things we've recovered from. Some of them of our own making. There are enough people who'll refuse to give up that the race will survive. Probably changed, unlikely any wiser, but enough of us will live. I plan to do everything I can to make sure we're a part of that group." Slowing, he turned down another road.

She thought on his words. "You might be right."

He started to speak, swearing instead as he swerved to avoid a group of people who ran out in front of them, their words impossible to understand with all of them shouting at once. "Hold on." He drove along the edge of the road, taking the next corner sharply.

Piper stared out the back, clinging to the edges of the seat. "What did they want?"

"Most likely to be rescued."

She faced forward, her mouth dropping open at the fire she could see ahead. They'd driven up a rise and could see large areas of the city in flames. "How much further do we need to go?"

"Nearly there. Try calling your parents again. See if they'll answer."

For a moment she feared they wouldn't. The second the call was connected, she spoke before anyone else could. "We're nearly there. Where are you?"

"In the same location," Alistair said.

Piper frowned, trying to figure out the tone of his voice.

"We'll be turning onto your road in less than a minute," Gibson said. "I'll flash my lights three times. You flash your lights twice then follow us."

When Alistair agreed, Piper recognised her dad's tone. "What happened? What's wrong?"

"We have two extra," Alistair said.

"We can't save the entire city." Gibson turned the corner, flashing his lights.

"They're toddlers," Tricia exclaimed. "A group hijacked their vehicle and shot the rest of the passengers. We couldn't leave them there."

Piper saw a parked vehicle flash its lights twice. "Was that your lights?"

"Yes," Alistair said.

"If those kids are infected, you might have killed everyone in your vehicle," Gibson said.

Piper could think of nothing to say and from the silence at the other end of the call, it seemed like she wasn't the only one. She watched as her parents pulled out onto the road, following them towards the fires. Before she could ask Gibson why he was taking them into danger, he turned down a street.

The rest of the trip back to the compound was silent, even though no one ended the call. Piper was tempted to ask what had happened to the toddlers and how they were managing to keep them quiet. But she didn't want to know. Didn't want to think about the ones that might have infected her and Selene's family. She frequently looked out the back window, making sure her family were following. Several times they needed to avoid vehicles left in the middle of the road, bodies scattered around them from what Piper assumed had been unsuccessful hijackings. There were also times when they had to drive around a single body left crumpled on the road.

Each time Piper looked away, not needing any extra images to add to the ones filling her mind. When they pulled up at the gates of the compound, she ended the call. "What are you doing? Why aren't we going inside?"

"We will, but they need to be cleaned up first and given masks to wear."

She took a deep breath before she got out of the vehicle, noticing both her and Selene's family were standing by their vehicle. The toddlers were nowhere in sight.

Tricia took half a step forward. "Piper?"

She nodded, walking towards her parents. "It's me."

"What are you wearing?" Alistair asked.

Gibson answered him. "It's to prevent us from becoming infected by Dawn. I need you to wear masks and to clean off any spores that might be on you. The compound is safe. We want to keep it that way."

Tricia took a step backwards. "Then we can't go inside the gates. I'm not going to risk Piper."

"Where is Selene?" Linda demanded.

"In quarantine where all of you will go." Gibson looked at each of them. "Except we don't have enough rooms for one each."

Selene's grandfather put his arm around his wife's shoulders. "We'll share a room."

Gibson nodded. "What happened to the toddlers?"

"We had to sedate them," Selene's grandmother said. "I used my sleeping medication. I called my doctor first. He recommended an appropriate dose."

"They wouldn't stop screaming," Linda said.

Selene's grandmother turned on her. "Could you expect anything else? They saw their family murdered."

Linda took a step back, holding up a hand. "Of course not. I was explaining what happened."

"We can talk about it later." Gibson looked past them. "I want to be inside before anyone has the chance to stumble across us."

It took longer than Piper expected for the vehicles to be cleaned out and parked in the area between the two fences where the outside was cleaned. There was just enough room for them to be parked side by side lengthwise in the area where they were left. Everyone was given medical masks and cleaned of any possible spores. It was made more difficult by the sleeping toddlers.

There were only five quarantine rooms and Selene and Wyatt were already using one. Selene's grandparents shared one room and Tricia volunteered to look after the toddlers. Piper protested, but Tricia was adamant that they couldn't be left alone. When Piper wanted to say Selene's grandparents or Linda could look after them, she turned away.

"I'll see if Emerson needs help." Piper almost ran inside, worried she'd make the suggestion. It would have been wrong. She'd known it was the moment she'd thought it, but she hadn't wanted to lose either of her parents.

Gibson found her an hour later, standing out the

front of the lab, staring up at the sky that was lightening, her protective gear left inside. She was tired, but there was no way she could sleep with the images that were invading her mind. She faced him when he stopped beside her. "Are they okay?"

"Emerson is happily taking blood and examining it, making notes in his files."

A reluctant smile formed, fading almost instantly. "Do you think they'll be okay?"

"It's too soon to tell." He slipped an arm around her shoulders, pulling her against his side. "You look exhausted."

"You don't look much better."

Gibson grinned. "Selene said something similar to me only a few minutes ago."

She turned her head, unable to meet his gaze. "How is she? And Wyatt?" She hadn't been able to face Selene after hearing her mum was to look after the toddlers. What if her friend was worse?

"I'm afraid I'm going to have to give you the same answer. It's too soon to tell."

Piper sighed heavily, not sure if she wanted to know when they'd be able to tell. It'd probably have her watching the time obsessively.

"You can stay at my place if you want a sleep."

She met his gaze. "How are fifty people meant to fit in here?"

"There are cottages out the back. The land slopes down gently so that they're hidden by the lab. Six more cottages. One is for Emerson, but he prefers the room he has at the lab."

"How are you meant to fit fifty people in six cottages?"

Gibson grinned. "They're bigger than mine and Zoe's. And that fifty also includes Zoe, Emerson and me." He paused a moment. "Did you want to have a sleep?"

"I should check on Selene."

"She's sleeping. Let her rest while she can." Gibson spoke again when Piper remained silent. "Emerson will call us if there are any changes. Someone needs to go outside and clear the scrub away from the fence tomorrow, before people find us. So the electrical current can work." He smiled. "I was hoping you might help."

"All right. I'll try and sleep." She paused a moment before she returned his smile. "And I'll try and help. Although I think tomorrow is already here." Not that she'd done anything like clearing away scrub before. The only plant she'd ever had dealings with was Dawn. Her smile faded.

"Come on." Gibson kept his arm around her as they walked to his cottage. "Did you want something to eat before you sleep?"

"No." She doubted she'd keep it down. Not with the images remaining in her head.

Gibson offered her the use of his bedroom, saying he'd sleep in the living room, and left her to prepare for bed. Piper was surprised that when she did lie down she fell instantly asleep. But she wasn't surprised to be woken several hours later from a bad dream, her heart racing and tears on her cheeks. She wiped them away, stumbling out of bed. There was no way she'd get any further sleep.

Chapter Twenty-Two

Stepping into the open plan kitchen and living room, Piper froze at the sight of Emerson who had broken off in mid sentence to Gibson. "Are my parents okay?" Her breath caught in her throat. "Is Selene?"

Emerson nodded. "It's the girl. The toddler. She's immune."

Piper looked from Emerson to Gibson, frowning. "How do you know?" Again her breath caught in her throat and she backed away, shaking her head. "Not my mum. She can't be infected."

"She's not showing signs of infection yet and the boy's immune system is fighting Dawn, but not doing as good a job as the girl's. We're giving him the drugs and he's showing signs of improvement," Emerson said. "They aren't siblings like I first thought. DNA testing shows that they're likely to be cousins."

"You can't leave my mum in there with them."

"She's wearing protective gear. Someone has to look after them and they respond well to her," Emerson said.

"No-"

Gibson came forward and captured her hand when she tried to step away from him. "We aren't going to do anything to hurt your family. Everything is being done to keep everyone safe."

"But the toddlers are infected." She couldn't get the images of the lungs filled with white threads from her mind. That couldn't happen to her mum.

"Only the boy and he wasn't far enough along to be contagious. If he was, everyone in the vehicle would have been infected. In a closed space like that no one would have had a chance to avoid contamination." Emerson checked the time. "I need to do the next lot of tests. Thought you might like to know. This is exciting news." He strode from the cottage.

Piper stared at the closed door. She'd wanted to ask Emerson questions. She turned to Gibson. "Why is it exciting news?"

"Emerson believes it's the first step to eliminating the infection. A preventative rather than a cure. He's been saying for months that there must be some who are naturally immune. Even though the plant doesn't come from our planet the odds are that someone will be immune to it."

"Why? Like you said, Dawn isn't from our planet."

"The kid would have been born after Dawn arrived on Earth. His theory is that one of her parents might have been involved with Dawn at some stage. But we'll never know."

She met his gaze. "The human race will survive." The words ran through her mind, chasing out some of the images. "You were right."

"It's too soon to tell."

His words brought a smile to her lips. "The human race will survive."

The cottage door burst open and Zoe strode inside. "You better not expect me to be the only one clearing outside the fence." Her hands went to her hips and she glared at her brother.

Gibson gestured towards the kitchen. "Do you want breakfast first?"

"I've had breakfast. But I will join you for lunch." Zoe closed the door, coming inside further. She looked towards Piper. "Your friend is improving. The drugs seem to be slowly killing off Dawn. Emerson plans to scan her and Wyatt's lungs later to see what's happening."

"Selene is getting better? She's going to survive?"

Zoe shrugged. "Wouldn't have a clue. This is the first time we've deliberately tried this method. Who knows what the success rate will be."

Gibson strode to the kitchen, taking out food and a pan. "We've had an accidental success rate of one hundred percent. Look at Jerome and Emerson. That counts for something."

The meal was spent with Gibson and Zoe arguing percentages, success rates and being more scientific about data. The argument was still going when Piper left to visit Selene, wanting to see for herself that her friend was improving. She closed the cottage door on Zoe's order not to take too long. They had a lot to get done before dark.

Piper stood at the door, looking through the glass pane at Selene and Wyatt. They both appeared to be asleep and she didn't know if she should wake them. While she was mentally debating the issue, Selene's eyes opened.

For a moment Selene's eyes remained unfocused, then she saw Piper and smiled. "Thank you." She struggled to sit up, disturbing Wyatt who looked around with confusion.

Piper frowned. "For what?"

"Bringing my family. Zoe told me."

"Of course I brought your family. You would have done the same for me."

There was a moment of silence before Selene spoke. "I'm sorry."

Again Piper was confused. "What for?"

"Letting Dawn flower. I should have listened to you."

"Selene, no." She pressed her hand against the glass. "It's not your fault. It's the ones who sold the plant who are to blame. Not you."

"But if I-"

"No. Dawn is spreading everywhere. Did you do that?"

Selene shook her head. "My mum would be alive if-"

"It's not your fault." Piper spoke the words fiercely. "Don't take the blame for the people who sold Dawn. Just don't. Only they deserve to be blamed."

Selene's eyes filled with tears. "Okay."

Wyatt wrapped an arm around Selene's shoulders. "I keep thinking there was something I should have done too. But there wasn't. We were doomed the moment they decided to sell the plants."

Piper thought of the toddler with an immunity to Dawn. "We aren't doomed. The human race will survive." Maybe not all of them, but Gibson was right. Many of them wouldn't give up and would keep looking for ways to win. "We'll evolve." She told them about the toddler.

"All the children born will be immune?" Wyatt asked.

"I don't think so. But some will and Emerson is working on a preventative as well as a cure." When neither seemed cheered by her words, Piper said, "Your family will be allowed out of quarantine at six tonight."

"Don't let them see me. Especially not my grandparents. Promise me, Piper." Selene struggled to rise to her feet, collapsing against Wyatt with a fit of coughing.

"They'll want to–"

"No. Not like this. Promise."

She had no idea how she was going to keep them away. "Okay." She paused a moment. "Hurry up and get well. I doubt I'll be able to keep them from you for long."

"You'll manage." Selene's eyes closed, her words sounding laboured. "I know you will."

Fear raced through Piper. She'd thought Selene was improving. Now she seemed worse than before. "I have to help Gibson and Zoe." She waited for Selene or Wyatt to reply. Neither did. After a few more seconds she hurried away, trying to push images of infected lungs from her mind. It didn't help. The images remained.

Zoe and Gibson waited outside the laboratory, with numerous tools, Zoe pacing back and forth. Both wore their protective gear. Zoe stopped pacing the moment Piper stepped outside. "About time."

Gibson handed protective gear to Piper. "We need to wear these every time we leave the compound."

She took them, pulling on the gear. It was going to be warm working outside in the protective gear. But far better than being infected by Dawn.

Gibson gathered up tools once Piper was dressed, handing them to her and Zoe, keeping some for himself. "Time to clear the fence line. Who wants to take first watch?" He held out a gun.

Piper took a step back, running into the door of the laboratory. "I've never used a gun."

Zoe took the gun from Gibson. "I will." She strode towards the gates muttering about dead weight.

Piper stared after Zoe. "Why do we need a gun?"

"People will do anything when their lives are at stake. Look what happened to the toddlers' family." Gibson gestured towards the gate. "We better get started."

Piper walked beside Gibson, trying not to think

about what she'd seen on the road when they'd collected her parents. As was becoming a habit, the images filled her mind anyway. No wonder she'd been woken by a nightmare.

Outside Zoe paced back and forth, watching for anyone who might come out of the scrub while Piper and Gibson worked on clearing the fence line. As Piper had expected, it was hot work, made worse by the protective gear she wore. Gibson took second watch and she had third. Taking the gun from Gibson, she held it carefully, listening as he explained how to use it.

"I hope it doesn't come to that because I don't know if I could shoot anyone." Piper stared at the gun in her hand.

Zoe took the gun from her. "If you were holding it properly I shouldn't have been able to take it so easily. Do you want to get us killed?"

"Of course I don't." She glared at Zoe. "This is new to me. I wouldn't have a clue what to do."

"Then I'll take this watch," Zoe said.

"She needs a break." Gibson stepped in front of Zoe when she started to move away.

"It's okay." Piper moved closer to Gibson. "She's right. I shouldn't be taking a turn watching when it might get us killed. I'm fine to keep working." Her arms ached and she felt like her protective gear had turned into a sauna, but that was nothing compared with dying. Or getting Gibson and Zoe killed.

Gibson turned to Piper. "If you're sure."

Zoe stepped around her brother. "You heard her. She's fine." Zoe returned to pacing the area nearby.

Piper nodded. "I'm fine. Let's get this fence line finished." The tools cut through the scrub quicker than she'd expected. The hardest part was dragging everything away from the fence. As the shadows lengthened, Piper paused to see what was left for them to do. Her shoulders slumped when she realised they were only half way. It looked like they'd need to spend tomorrow outside clearing the fence too.

"Don't come any closer."

At Zoe's warning, Piper spun to see what was happening.

Chapter Twenty-Three

Piper stared at the group of people who had come out of the trees, raising their hands, three children of varying ages with them. There were four men and two women. They dropped sticks that were solid enough to be used as weapons.

"We don't mean any harm," one of the men said. "We're looking for somewhere safe. We have children with us."

Piper almost pointed out that their oldest child wasn't much younger than her. Only three or four years younger.

"What are your skills?" Zoe demanded.

The man who'd addressed them gestured towards the older man of their group. "Dad is the only one with any skills. When he was younger he was a labourer on one of those organic farms that did things the old fashioned way. With human labour rather than robotics."

Zoe glanced towards Piper. "See. Someone who can pull their own weight."

Piper wanted to argue that she had been pulling her weight today. But the group of strangers remained in front of them and she had no idea what they might do. "All the quarantine rooms are full."

"Some might be empty at six." Gibson glanced skywards. "Must be less than two hours away by now."

"We'll only have space for three at the most," Zoe said.

"Take our children. As long as the children are safe-" one of the women started to say.

Zoe interrupted her. "We don't need more dead weight."

"I'm not about to save myself at the expense of my grandchildren," the older man said.

"The kids could go in one room and the adults split between the other two rooms," Piper suggested.

"And what if only one of them is infected and kills off the rest?" Zoe demanded.

"The children first," the older man insisted.

"They can wear medical masks while they wait to

find out," Piper said. If the human race was to survive then as many of them as possible needed to be saved.

"How long does it take?" the first man asked.

"Twelve hours to be certain," Gibson said.

The other middle aged man gestured towards the compound. "How do we know it's any better in there than out here?"

Two men and a woman came out of the trees to the left of the group in front of Piper. The woman carried a gun, the men with her carried crowbars. The woman pointed the gun at Zoe. "If they don't want to go in, we do. In fact, I think all of you should stay out here and we go in there." She nodded towards the compound.

Piper couldn't look away from the gun the woman held. Surely Zoe wasn't going to give into the woman's demands. The other group had backed away, pushing their children behind them. Piper wished she could back away too, but the fence prevented her.

Zoe lowered her gun. "If we let you in, you have to promise not to shoot us."

The woman laughed. "Sure. We can promise that." She glanced at the two men with her. "Right, guys?"

They laughed, nodding in agreement.

Fear raced through Piper. Her parents were in the

compound, locked in quarantine rooms. She started to take a step forward, opening her mouth to protest.

Gibson intercepted her, wrapping his arms around her. "It's okay. They won't hurt us if we let them in the compound." His arms tightened momentarily. "Don't move." He met her gaze for a moment before letting go and stepping away. "I'll let you in." He strode towards the gate, using the keypad to unlock it and stepping back. "Remember your promise." He gestured towards the open gate.

Piper clasped her hands together, wanting to run ahead and let her parents out. Her gaze was drawn to the gun. She remained where she was.

Grinning, the woman strode towards the open gate. "Don't you try anything or I will shoot." The two men followed her.

"We wouldn't think of it." Zoe continued to hold the gun at her side.

The woman glanced at her before stepping through the gate. The woman's face was twisted by pain and she screamed, dropping the gun as the two men ran into her, both screaming as they dropped their crowbars. The three of them staggered back, their weapons left in the area between the two fences.

Zoe raised her gun, pointing it at the woman.

"Back away from the compound or I will shoot." Her voice was hard, her hand steady.

Piper stared open mouthed at the woman and two men. What had happened to them? How had Gibson and Zoe managed it?

The woman staggered away from the fence. "You wait. I'll get even for that."

Zoe shrugged. "If you live long enough. Now walk and keep walking."

Piper watched the three of them head back through the trees and out of sight. "They'll come back."

Gibson closed the gate. "It won't help them. They won't live long enough to return. Either they'll attack the wrong person or Dawn will infect them."

The first group came forward, the older man at the front. "How do you get inside?"

"Through the gate," Zoe said. "But only those we allow inside." She glanced around. "We've got work to do."

"We'll help." The older man stepped forward. "I'm Caden." He made a sweeping gesture to those with him. "My son and daughters and their husbands and children."

"It won't guarantee you'll be able to come in," Gibson said.

"All we ask is that you take the children," Caden said.

"You'd be more useful than the kids." Zoe glanced at Caden before returning to scanning the area for trouble.

Caden shrugged. "Why not see what we're capable of?"

Gibson nodded.

Piper watched for a moment as the group came forward and removed what they'd cut away. After a couple of minutes she returned to cutting back the encroaching plants. Things went faster with the extra help and eventually Gibson let one of the men help cut away the plants since they were standing around waiting for more to be cut. As darkness fell, Zoe handed a spotlight to the youngest child to shine on the workers while she held another spotlight and used it to scan the area.

They arrived back at the gate, the second part of the job done in a fraction of the time. Zoe kept hold of the gun, continuing to scan the area with her spotlight. "We can shut you in the space between the two fences if you want. It might be safer than staying outside. Those other three might still be in the area."

Gibson unlocked the gate, stepping inside to gather up the weapons. Along with the tools he carried, he cleaned off any possible spores on them and himself before gesturing everyone to enter.

"Thanks." One of the women ushered the children into the area, followed by the rest of her family.

The outer gate was shut and the inner one not opened until everyone was cleaned off and the group had donned medical masks. Piper stared at them a moment before she followed Gibson to the laboratory, Zoe having strode to her cottage. The hope in their eyes had her hurrying away. What if there was no room for them? What if her or Selene's family were infected? Her chest tightened and her steps slowed. She couldn't bear it if anything happened to her parents.

Gibson looked over his shoulder before he entered the laboratory. "Are you coming?"

"Yeah." She caught up with him and waited in the lab while he set the weapons and tools to the side.

"We can put everything away later." He began to remove his protective gear. "I thought you might like to check on your parents first."

She did and she didn't. "Yeah." She started to remove her protective gear.

"They'll be okay. Even your mum." Gibson put the protective gear near the other items he'd brought inside.

Finished taking off her gear, she tried to smile. It barely formed, fading as the fear overwhelmed her. What if they weren't okay? And what about Selene? What if she didn't survive?

Gibson took a step towards her. "I'll-"

The door leading further into the building opened, interrupting Gibson. Emerson entered the room. "I was wondering when you'd be in here. I'm about to release most of them."

"Who?" Piper clasped her hands together, but it didn't stop the tremble in them.

"Only Tricia and the boy will be left in quarantine. And Selene and Wyatt of course," Emerson said.

"Oh."

"The rest of them should be out by tomorrow."

Piper stared at Emerson. "Everyone? Selene too?"

Emerson nodded. "The boy is healing at a good rate. Your mum isn't infected, but has elected to care for the boy and the other two are healing at a remarkable rate. Once their temperatures were high and the drugs started to work that is. We've also managed to keep their temperatures from rising too high."

A smile slowly formed. "They're going to be all right?"

Emerson nodded. "And it looks like you can't get

reinfected. I've tried to reinfect the rats that survived, but it won't take."

"We can let them out now?" Piper felt giddy with relief.

Emerson nodded.

"That's good." Gibson grinned. "We've got a handful of people between the fences waiting to be admitted to quarantine."

Piper interrupted when Emerson started to question Gibson. "What about my dad and Selene's family? We can answer questions later. Everyone is waiting to be let out." Nor could she wait another minute.

Gibson chuckled. "Come on. I'll help you let them out and Zoe can sort out the people between the fences and answer Emerson's questions." He looked towards Emerson. "Call Zoe and let her know." He led the way to the quarantine rooms.

Chapter Twenty-Four

Piper looked through the glass panel of the door at her dad, tears filling her eyes. He sat on the bed, his head resting in his hands. "Dad." The word was spoken low, but it was loud enough that he raised his head.

He stared at Piper for a moment before rising to his feet and rushing to the door. "Piper. You're okay?"

She nodded, wiping away tears. The moment the door was open she threw herself into his arms. "You're okay too. Your tests came back clear."

"What about your mother?"

"She's okay, but she's staying with the boy until tomorrow."

"Can I see her?" Alistair turned to Gibson, keeping an arm around Piper. "Can I see my wife?"

"Of course you can." Gibson led the way, leaving Alistair to talk to Tricia through the door.

The girl refused to leave her cousin, clinging to him when they said she could come out. They left her in the room and Alistair in the corridor while they let out Selene's family. Linda was adamant that she needed to see her niece. Remembering Selene's request, Piper argued with her. Eventually she had to tell them Selene was ill and needed plenty of rest if she was to recover. But she was recovering.

Once everyone was settled, Piper returned to Gibson's cottage with him. Selene's family were in one of the cottages, the group that had waited in the area between the fences were in the three contamination rooms and Alistair remained in the corridor talking to Tricia.

She helped Gibson make sandwiches, trying to ignore her aching muscles. "How did you stop that woman, with the gun, from entering?"

"There are two codes you need to use to enter the compound. If you only use the first one whoever comes in is hit with a jolt of electricity. Not high enough to kill, but enough to hurt."

Zoe entered the cottage before Piper could ask further questions. "I was talking to Linda and her parents. They might actually be useful. She's a history teacher. Knows how things were done before machinery and robotics."

Piper tried not to smile. "I guess I'm the only dead weight around here."

Gibson set the food on the bench and slid his arm around her waist, drawing her close. "You did a lot of work today considering you're dead weight."

"Oh shut up," Zoe muttered. She gestured towards the food. "Any for me?"

"If you want some," Gibson said.

"I do." Zoe helped prepare the sandwiches and when they were eating, said, "We're going to have to think about doing food runs now we're getting more people here. We don't want to start on our supplies any sooner than we have to. Food will eventually become scarce before things have any chance of getting better."

"Where will you get food from?" Piper asked.

"Where there's the most Dawn. No one else will be in those areas. Or at least less people will be."

Piper stared at Gibson. Surely she'd misheard him. "But Dawn will be there."

"You don't have to come with us," Zoe said.

Zoe's tone made Piper want to argue with her. Ignoring Zoe, Piper faced Gibson. "Won't it be dangerous?"

"Less dangerous than working outside the compound."

Piper shuddered at Gibson's words. She hadn't expected to live through that encounter. "What about the spores?"

"We'll wear protective gear and only take glass jars and tinned items." Gibson glanced at Zoe, his gaze returning to Piper. "We've spent a lot of time working everything out. We knew what would happen. This is the safest option."

"You going with us?" Zoe demanded.

She looked from one to the other, eventually nodding. She wasn't about to let Zoe accuse her of being dead weight again. "What time will we leave?"

"Before daybreak. Things should be quieter." Zoe finished off the last of her sandwich, rising to her feet. "I'll see you in the morning."

Piper watched Zoe stride from the cottage. She wouldn't be there when her mum came out of quarantine. Taking a deep breath, she faced Gibson. "What do I need to take?"

"We've got everything organised."

"Okay." Finishing off her sandwich, she felt extremely unprepared. Dawn wasn't meant to be like this.

Gibson rose from the table. "I'll clean up if you want to go to bed. I borrowed a change of clothes from Zoe for you. They're in the bathroom."

"Thanks." She sat at the table for a few more seconds before she retreated to the bathroom and readied herself for bed. When she climbed into Gibson's bed, she lay awake far too long listening to him in the living area, trying to push the many nightmare images from her mind. Eventually she managed to fall asleep.

When Gibson woke Piper, she felt tired and her body ached from yesterday's unaccustomed exercise. "What time is it?" She looked up at him silhouetted by the light coming through the bedroom door.

"About two hours until the sun rises." Gibson fell silent for a moment. "Do you want breakfast?"

"Yeah." Yawning, she covered her mouth. "I'll be out in a minute."

"Okay." Gibson left the room, closing the bedroom door three quarters of the way.

Stumbling out of bed, she stifled another yawn. It didn't take her long to use the bathroom and join Gibson at the table. "I need more clothes." She couldn't keep borrowing Zoe's. They were a size too big.

"We can get some today."

"How?"

"By taking them from the empty shops. You won't be able to try anything on, but as long as everything has the spores frozen, and is made from natural fibres, you can take it."

She stared at him a moment, her fork halfway to her mouth. "We're going to steal from shops?"

Gibson chuckled. "How did you think we were going to get food?"

She placed the fork on her plate. "I don't know. But I hadn't expected that. I mean…" Her voice trailed off. She had no idea about anything anymore.

"Life is different. It'll never be the same." Gibson's voice was soft.

"I didn't expect it to be. I just…" She shrugged. "I don't know. It seems wrong to steal."

"Think of it as going on a scavenger hunt. A survival scavenger hunt."

"I'll try."

Gibson nodded to Piper's plate. "Eat up. Zoe will be here any minute."

Piper had barely managed another mouthful when Zoe burst inside followed by Linda as well as Caden's son, the youngest adult of Caden's group. She hurriedly ate the rest of the food as she rose from the table, heading to the kitchen sink with her plate.

Zoe jerked her head towards her companions. "They're coming with us." She looked between Piper and Gibson. "You pair ready?"

Piper left her plate beside the sink. "Yes." She wasn't about to hold them up. Zoe would probably complain about it for months.

"Then let's go." Zoe strode outside, leaving the door open, Linda following her.

Caden's son remained inside, holding out his hand. "We weren't officially introduced yesterday. I'm Haleb."

Gibson stepped forward to shake his hand, followed by Piper.

"Thanks for letting me come along," Haleb said. "You won't regret letting my family stay here."

Zoe stepped back inside. "I'm waiting. We want to be deep in the city by daylight."

Piper followed Zoe outside, stopping when she saw the vehicle parked near the gate. It was different to the other ones, reminding her of the military vehicles that were taken into hostile areas. Her breath caught in her throat and she opened her mouth several times before she managed to speak. "It looks like we're going to war."

Zoe opened the rear door, handing out protective gear. "We are. Dawn is the enemy. I don't know how they could have expected to bring an alien here without wondering if it would take over. We pretty much handed our world to it."

Chapter Twenty-Five

Once Piper was dressed, she clambered in the back of the vehicle with Linda and Haleb. Seats ran lengthwise, the area between the back seats and the front ones filled with a cage containing weapons, tools and a solid backpack with a lengthy hose that she was told would be used to freeze Dawn. Soft lighting was in the ceiling in the back, very little of it filtering into the front of the vehicle.

The drive was silent. Piper stared out the darkened windows in the back, as did Linda and Haleb. Her city was barely recognisable. Large areas had been burned, smoke drifting out of some of the buildings. Numerous vehicles littered the roads, bodies scattered around them. Piper looked away. She couldn't watch any longer. It was a surprise to look outside again and see Dawn climbing up buildings, across the road and partially hiding dead bodies.

"How did they think they could get away with releasing Dawn?" Linda's words were soft, as if she didn't expect an answer.

"Greed can convince people of many things," Zoe said. "They knew, but they thought others were as greedy as them."

Gibson pulled up beside a multi-story shopping complex. The only sign of life was Dawn. The plant crept over the building like it was a trellis. "Don't get out until the air inside the vehicle has been adjusted."

"Adjusted to what?" Haleb asked.

"To freeze any spores that might get inside," Zoe said.

They sat in silence, looking out the windows, the sun now above the horizon, glimpses of it seen between buildings. Everywhere Piper looked, she saw Dawn. Vivid green tear shaped leaves, vines clambering over every surface, bell shaped flowers at various stages of growth and dandelion like fluff floating on the air.

"Time to get out," Gibson said.

Once everyone was out of the vehicle, Zoe handed out weapons, keeping the backpack for freezing Dawn for herself. She picked up a spotlight. Gibson handed out large string bags and grabbed a wrecking bar for himself.

Piper eyed the bag. It was going to take awhile to fill it. She glanced around the area. The place remained deserted. "How are we going to get inside?"

Zoe laughed. "My favourite method." She aimed the hose at the nearby plants, freezing them to create a pathway.

Gibson locked the vehicle before following his sister. "Come on. We don't want to remain around here any longer than necessary."

Piper hurried after him. She didn't want to stay around here any longer than necessary either. It felt like another planet. An eerie, deserted one. When a tendril reached towards her, she picked up her pace. Once she'd thought that adorable. Now it felt menacing.

"Can't we freeze the plants and take back our city?" Haleb asked.

"It's not only our city. This is what every city on our planet currently looks like. Unless they live in climates that are below zero degrees Celsius," Zoe said.

"If we moved to a country with year round snow we'd be safe?" Linda asked.

"Yeah." Zoe froze another plant.

"I hate the cold. Why couldn't it have been the heat," Linda muttered.

"I'm with you there," Haleb said. "A nice tropical island, fishing all day, sleeping under the stars of a night."

"There's ice fishing." Gibson pried open the door of the shopping complex with the wrecking bar.

Haleb followed Gibson inside. "Somehow it doesn't have the same ring as fishing on a tropical island."

"Do you think there are islands that are safe?" Piper cautiously entered the building, relieved when Zoe turned on the spotlight.

Gibson glanced at her before walking further into the building. "The spore can travel really long distances on the slightest of breezes."

"Dawn doesn't need soil to grow. It can live on anything. Including debris floating on the water, as long as it's synthetic. We have a lot of rubbish in our oceans. Dawn flourishes in any environment above fifteen degrees Celsius. Struggles to grow at temperatures below that and dies at zero degrees." Zoe continued to lead the way, their footsteps echoing through the empty building.

There were fewer plants inside, the amount less the further into the shopping complex they went. Piper kept looking around, too many shadows for her liking. Anything could be hiding. "Are we going somewhere in particular?"

"We're after supermarkets." Zoe shone the spotlight at the various shopfronts.

Piper looked at the many familiar names, realising where she was. The shopping complex where Selene had purchased Dawn. A shiver went through her and her grip tightened on the gun. Her steps slowed. It was out the front of this building that she'd first met Gibson. Her gaze was drawn to him.

He glanced over his shoulder. "Is something wrong? You need to keep up." He dropped back to walk beside her. "There might be people in here."

"We met out the front of this shopping complex."

Gibson didn't reply to Piper immediately. "I know." His smile was visible in his eyes, his mouth hidden by the protective gear. "It's one of the few good things that have come from Dawn."

"Few? What else is good about Dawn's arrival?"

"People coming together to help each other. I know not everyone will, but Zoe and I have already seen people working together to try and eradicate Dawn," Gibson said.

Zoe glanced over her shoulder. "I'm sorry to say my brother has always been this lame. There's nothing good about Dawn. It killed our father and now it plans to take our world."

"Dawn isn't all that has killed friends and family," Haleb said. "People can be equally cruel."

A sound drew their attention and Zoe shone the spotlight towards it.

"Stop there. Don't come any further. Who are you?" An elderly man waved a gun, the frames of his glasses covered in white, thread-like roots that stretched out over some of the glass. Beside him was a young dog, her brindle coat shiny, her muzzle covered by medical masks that were tied together.

Piper took a step backwards. The gun looked like it belonged in a museum and was as likely to kill the one firing it as the one it was being aimed at.

The man took off his glasses, pushing the threads to the side before he put them on again. "Who are you?"

"We're looking for food. Lower your gun. We have no plans to hurt you," Gibson said.

"Food? Waste of time. We're doomed." The man coughed, blood coating his palm. He wiped his hand across the side of his trousers and patted his dog when she whined.

Gibson took a step towards the man. "Not everyone is doomed. We live in a compound were Dawn can't enter."

The man glanced over his shoulder, pressing a finger to his lips. He shuffled forward. "Don't tell them. They take everything. Wanted my dog. Not about to let them eat her. Nothing wrong with tinned food."

"Who wants to eat her?" Piper stared at the dog in horror. Why would anyone want to eat a dog?

"Sounds like it's time to get out of here," Linda said.

"Not without food," Zoe stated.

"Are there other people in here?" Gibson asked the man.

He nodded, indicating over his shoulder. "Five of them. Think this place is theirs. Holed up in the bigger supermarket." He looked from his dog to Gibson. "You want to safely find food, I can tell you. But only if you take my dog. You save her and I'll save you a run in with that crazy bunch."

Zoe stepped up beside Gibson. "No. You can't save everyone."

"She might not be infected. She looks pretty healthy," Gibson said.

"No. We'll find the food on our own." Zoe gestured towards the dog. "She'll take up space and be of no use."

"She's a good dog. Loyal and smart," the man argued.

"We're not taking her." Zoe faced Gibson. "Get that look out of your eyes."

Piper wanted to argue with Zoe that surely saving one dog wouldn't matter. But knew it was pointless. About the only one she'd listen to was Gibson.

"What's her name?" Gibson asked.

"Pie. My grandson named her. Said she was better than pie." The old man chuckled, ending up coughing again.

An ache formed in Piper's chest. "This isn't right. We should be trying to save them both." How could the human race survive if they didn't help everyone they could?

Zoe spun to face Piper. "We can't save everyone. There isn't room at the compound. Don't you get it? Resources are limited, safe areas are limited and who knows how long it'll take us to get rid of Dawn. It could take generations. If the human race lives that long."

"She's right." The old man nodded towards Zoe. "I'm too old to be worth saving. But Pie isn't. She's worth ten of any human."

Linda glanced around the area. "We can't stand here all day. There are other people in here somewhere. Let's get what we came for and get out."

Piper continued to meet Zoe's gaze. "He's wrong.

So are you. If we rescue people only because of what they can do for us, we're as bad as the ones who sold Dawn for profit."

"I'm nothing like them," Zoe snarled.

"Aren't you?" Piper held her ground when Zoe took a step towards her.

"No." Zoe waved a hand towards the old man. "How will you feel if we take him in and there's no room for someone who can make a difference? For the person who might discover a way to get rid of Dawn."

Chapter Twenty-Six

Piper refused to back down. Zoe was wrong. Picking and choosing wasn't the way to survive. "How do you know he isn't that person? Who knows what experiences he has that will help." Piper looked towards the man. "What's your name?"

"Freddie."

"Don't you want to live, Freddie?"

He shrugged. "I've done my living. Now if I could get to my family and make sure they lived, that'd be a different matter altogether."

Piper stared at him for a moment. "How can you save them if you don't live?"

Before Freddie could speak, the sound of footsteps came towards them, lights bobbing up and down as five men came around a corner, a spotlight in one hand and a gun in the other. They wore medical masks, the lower half of their faces hidden.

The one in the lead spoke. "Who you got with you, Freddie? Looks like they have some gear we could use." He pointed his gun at Gibson, who was at the front of the group.

Freddie threw himself at the man who'd pointed his gun at Gibson, forcing the gun upwards before it was fired. When Freddie was knocked to the floor, Pie attacked the man, unable to do much through the masks tied over her muzzle.

When the man laughed and tried to kick Pie, Zoe aimed the hose at him. "Back off, now."

The men laughed, aiming their weapons at Zoe, the one in the lead taking a step towards her.

"I warned you." Zoe strode forwards, sending the freezing mist at the five men, most of it aimed at the one who'd gone for Pie.

The men staggered backwards, stumbling over each other, yelling and threatening Zoe.

Gibson came forward and gathered up their spotlights and weapons. "Stop, Zoe. Before you kill them."

Zoe lowered the hose, glancing at Piper. "Told you most people aren't worth rescuing."

"Some people aren't, not most," Piper said firmly.

Haleb kept his gun trained on the men. "What are we going to do with them?"

Gibson turned off the men's spotlights, putting them in his string bag before checking the safety on each gun and adding them to the bag. "There has to be somewhere we can put them while we get what we came for."

Freddie took the hand Gibson held out to him, getting to his feet. "A corridor further along this way." He indicated the direction he'd come from. "The doors can be closed and something put through the handles so they'll have to find their way in the dark to the other end. Should slow them down enough for you to get done in here."

The man who'd been in the lead held his hands at his mouth, breathing on them. "You better hope we don't find you before you get out of here."

Zoe pointed the hose at him. "Need more of this?"

The man glared at her, but remained silent.

Freddie showed them where the corridor was and they jammed the door shut, walking away to the accompaniment of the men's threats. "Want me to show you where the supermarket is?" He jerked a thumb towards the door. "Might want to get out of here before that lot find you."

"We didn't agree to take you or your dog," Zoe warned.

Freddie nodded. "I know." He headed down the corridor, glancing over his shoulder. "You coming?"

Zoe strode after Freddie. "We can't take everyone."

"I know."

"I'm serious," Zoe said.

Smiling, Piper followed them, Zoe continuing to argue that they couldn't take them while Freddie kept reassuring her he knew. She glanced at Gibson, who walked beside her, seeing the humour in his eyes. Keeping her voice low, so Zoe couldn't hear her, she asked, "Are we taking them?"

Gibson glanced at his sister before he nodded.

Relief rushed through Piper and she caught up with Zoe, determined to get out of the shopping complex before the men escaped and found them.

At the supermarket they filled their bags with tinned food, various sized clothing made from natural fibres and food packaged in glass jars. Passing the confectionery aisle, Piper sighed. All the chocolate was in plastic wrappers. They couldn't risk that it was contaminated by Dawn. Nor were the freezers running. Rows of ice cream and goods no longer edible.

Back out at the vehicle they stored everything in the freezing cold interior, Freddie having shown them a shortcut to the front of the building. Zoe turned to her brother. "Get out the insulated body bag." She pointed a finger at him. "And get that smile off your face. I can see it in your eyes."

"What is the body bag for?" Linda asked. "We're not taking any dead people back with us, are we?"

"Of course we aren't," Zoe snapped. "It's so we don't freeze anyone we take with us. There's no point in cleaning anyone here. The spores will be back on them in seconds."

"You're taking Pie with you?" Freddie asked.

"As if she'd stay in the bag on her own." Zoe spread the long, white bag out on the ground, opening it. "Come on. Get in. We don't have all day."

"But…" Freddie looked at each of them. "I'm old and dying. There's nothing I can help you with." He began to cough, blood coating his hand. When he finished coughing, he slowly shook his head. "You're wasting your time. Get out there and save someone worth saving."

"Get in the bag or I'm leaving Pie behind." Zoe put one hand on her hip, the other holding the hose.

Freddie looked at each of them once more before lying in the bag, Pie joining him to snuggle into his side. He wrapped an arm around his dog, whispering reassurances to her while Zoe closed the bag.

Gibson and Haleb came forward to help Zoe lift

Freddie into the vehicle. Piper clambered in once Zoe had put her backpack away and went around to the front of the vehicle. It was a quiet trip to the compound and Piper spent more time looking at the body bag on the floor than looking out the window. The couple of times she'd looked outside had shown her buildings that Dawn was starting to devour. Ones built from manmade materials.

Arriving back, the vehicle was parked in the area between the two fences, both it and the occupants being cleaned before they entered the compound. Piper walked inside, unable to watch Freddie thank Zoe over and over again, half the time telling her she'd made a mistake saving him, having put on a medical mask to prevent spores escaping from his lungs. She'd left her gear behind in the vehicle, glad to finally be out of it. When she saw her parents coming towards her, walking around the side of the laboratory building, her steps slowed. Neither of them looked impressed.

"We had expected you to be here when I got out of quarantine," Tricia said.

"Everyone has to pull their weight around here." Piper was almost grateful to Zoe that she was able to say that.

"You're a child. It's different," Alistair protested.

"No it's not."

Piper turned to see Zoe striding towards them. She glanced around. "Where are Freddie and Pie?"

"Gibson and Haleb are taking them to Emerson." Zoe faced Alistair. "We didn't have to bring you here. We could have left you out there." She waved a hand towards the gate. "If you don't like the way we do things, you're welcome to leave." She paused a moment. "Everyone pulls their weight. Including kids as soon as they're able. Jobs will be assigned to everyone. If you have no skills, then you're on whatever job you're given."

"It's dangerous out there," Tricia said.

Zoe glared at Tricia. "You think that means you lot get to stay safely in here while the rest of us risk our lives for you? That you're somehow better than us?"

Tricia shook her head. "I didn't mean that. We can go outside. Let the children stay in the compound."

"No." Piper nearly took a step back when everyone turned to face her. "I'm not a child. I'll take my turn going outside the compound like everyone else." Tricia tried to hug Piper, but she stepped away. "Life is different, Mum." Her words were soft, but firm. She wasn't about to let everyone else risk their life for her. "I can do this." She smiled. "Have done this."

Tricia's eyes filled with tears and this time when

she tried to hug Piper, she was able to. "I was terrified something would happen to you. When you turned off your device and we didn't hear from you for so long, we expected the worst. Especially when it was all over the news about Dawn killing people."

"I'm okay." Piper tried to pull away, but her mum's arms tightened around her. "Other than I can't breathe." Seeing Zoe walk away, she was tempted to call her back and beg her to give her a job. Any job. "Mum."

Alistair put his arm across their shoulders. "We're staying in a cottage with Selene's family. Her grandmother is making lunch. You're probably hungry."

Hearing her friend's name, Piper froze. "How is Selene? And Wyatt."

"They're both at the cottage. Weak, but on the mend." Tricia finally let go of Piper. "I'm sure she'll want to see you."

Piper smiled. Obviously her mum was looking for ways to entice her to safety. "Lunch sounds good and I can't wait to see Selene." She walked beside her parents, looking around the area behind the laboratory. It looked different from inside the fence. She'd only seen it from outside when she'd helped clear the fence line.

The cottage Piper entered was similar to Gibson's, only larger and with more doors leading off the open plan living area. Her gaze was drawn to Selene, propped up on a couch beside Wyatt. A grin formed at the sight of her friend and she was across the room in seconds, both talking at once.

Wyatt moved over so Piper could squeeze in between them. Shaking his head and smiling when Piper said it wasn't necessary. "If I had the energy I'd move. There's no way I can ever thank you for saving my life."

Piper felt uncomfortable. She almost said it was nothing, then realised that of course it was something. And telling him 'you're welcome' seemed rather lame. "Uhm…"

Selene giggled. "Don't worry. We're not going to fawn over you and I'm not about to treat you any different." She slipped an arm around Piper's shoulders. "But I am going to have to thank you at least once for bringing my family here."

Piper couldn't stop smiling. She'd been terrified Selene wouldn't make it. "Okay. As long as it's only once."

"Lunch is ready," Linda called out.

There was a lot of noise as everyone relocated to the table, Alistair and Linda helping Selene and

Wyatt over. The toddlers were at the table too, along with Selene's grandparents. The meal was noisy and everyone was full of questions that Piper didn't want to answer. The city was nothing like it had once been and far worse than it had been when they'd escaped. Dawn was rapidly taking over. Soon only the colder areas would be free of her presence. And Australia didn't have enough cold areas. Too much of the country was in a Tropical zone.

Chapter Twenty-Seven

Late afternoon, while Selene and Wyatt had a nap, Piper escaped the endless questions by saying she was needed at the laboratory. She entered to find Zoe talking to Pie. The dog was in one of the larger quarantine boxes Emerson used for his experiments.

Zoe glared at Piper. "She was whining. Don't know how anyone can expect me to work with that noise."

Piper barely managed to hide a smile. "Need a hand with anything?"

"No. Go help Gibson. He's at his place, storing the clothes in his spare built-in wardrobe."

"Okay." Piper headed outside, her grin escaping. She was still smiling when she reached Gibson's cottage and knocked on the door.

He opened the door and stepped back so she could enter. "You don't need to knock."

"Thanks." She stepped inside. "Zoe said you might need help putting clothes away."

"I've finished."

"Your sister isn't as tough as she acts, is she?"

Gibson shook his head. "Like I said, she's terrified of losing more people she cares about. Dad's death hit her the hardest. She kept thinking there was something she could do. She worked hours in the lab trying to figure it out."

"What about you?"

"I know who's to blame and it wasn't any of us. It was those who wanted to risk everyone's life to save their own. Who originally thought they could make a profit and asked those they shouldn't have when no one else could see the profit in the plant."

"Oh." She had no idea what to say to him.

Gibson grinned. "What say we forget about the world coming to an end, alien invaders and evil corporations and pretend that life is normal and you watch a movie with me? Something with a happy ending."

"Like a date?"

"Yes. Like a date. If we wait until we finish dealing with Dawn, we might be old and grey. And you were the one who suggested a movie. So what do you say?"

She moved closer to him. "I'd love to." Smiling,

she made her way to the couch when he gestured to it, leaning against him when he sat beside her after putting a movie on. It felt so normal. He slipped his arm around her shoulders and his warmth against her side was not only comforting, but reminded her of when life had been normal. Back before Dawn.

Not wanting to lose the feeling of normality, Piper suggested another movie once the first one was finished, falling asleep partway through it. She woke to find Zoe perched on the end of the couch. Sitting up, she rubbed her eyes, looking around for Gibson. Night must have fallen because there was a light on.

"He's not here. Told me to wait with you so you didn't wake alone."

"He could have left a note." She'd have to let him know that waking up alone was preferable to waking up to his sister glaring at her. "Where did he go?"

Zoe continued to glare at her. "You keep inviting people in. Dead weight. You can't keep doing that. You're endangering all of us."

Fear raced through her and she stood up. "What happened? Where's Gib?"

Zoe stood up too. "Gibson and Emerson are all I have left. If we keep taking in people who can't help, I might lose them too."

She wanted to shake Zoe. "Where is Gib?"

"Freddie died."

"Oh." Pain washed over her. She'd wanted him to live. After all the arguing and getting Zoe to give in, she'd wanted him to live so he could prove to Zoe that everyone had potential. Taking a deep breath, she met Zoe's gaze. "I'm sorry." She'd keep pushing until Zoe learned that everyone deserved a chance to prove themselves. An image of the woman who'd held them at gunpoint and the men who'd wanted to eat Pie came to mind. Well, most people deserved a chance.

"He was dead when we took him in."

"If we don't take in everyone we can, Emerson and Gib might be all you end up with. You think you can live in a world with only three people?"

"You haven't lost anyone. You don't know what it's like."

"Maybe not, but I can imagine. I don't think a world without humanity would be a place worth living in." She had only to think about the many times she'd feared for her parents' lives recently to know what it would be like to lose them.

Zoe held out a piece of paper.

Frowning, Piper took it, looking at what appeared to be a hand drawn map. "What is this?"

"Where Freddie's family is."

Piper looked from the map to Zoe. "I don't understand."

"His daughter is a surgeon. She takes two weeks off every year to stay at the family farm and spend time with her two children. Freddie was due to pick her up yesterday. They're about an hour from here."

She almost couldn't bring herself to ask. "We're going to get them?"

"A surgeon is useful." Zoe took the map from her, remaining silent for a few seconds. "I guess Freddie was too." She strode towards the front door.

Piper stood in stunned silence for a moment before she hurried after Zoe. "When are we going? I can go too?"

Zoe turned to point a finger at Piper. "This doesn't mean we're going to rescue every single person we come across."

Piper tried not to smile. "Of course not. It'd be crazy to rescue anyone who held us at gunpoint."

Zoe glared at her. "Say another word and you're staying at the compound. We leave tonight. As soon as Gibson and Haleb are back."

Piper pressed her lips together, barely managing not to comment. Or grin. Once she had herself under control, she said, "Give me ten minutes to get ready."

Zoe nodded and slipped outside, closing the door.

Piper grinned, having caught a glimpse of Pie waiting for Zoe, wagging her tail the moment the girl stepped outside, Zoe's hand brushing across the dog's head. Piper's smile faded. She didn't want to end up like Zoe. Terrified to care because she'd lost too many to Dawn. She had no idea how to prevent that from happening. There were going to be losses. The image of the thread filled lungs filled her mind. She pushed it aside, thinking of Selene and Wyatt. But there'd also be people saved.

Not wanting to be left behind, she raided the clothes they'd brought back from the shopping complex, glad to change into something that fit properly. Outside she found Zoe waiting by the military vehicle, her arms crossed over her chest, Pie leaning against her leg.

Piper glanced around the area that was lit by spotlights. "Are they back yet?"

Zoe pushed away from the vehicle. "Does it look like it?" She glanced at the dog. "Come on. You need to stay with Emerson." She strode towards the laboratory.

Piper stared after her, not sure what to do. A sound had her spinning to face the gate. Relief rushed through her when she saw Gibson and Haleb enter the compound, wearing their protective gear. Gibson carried a flamethrower while Haleb had the freezing backpack.

Gibson strode towards Piper. "You heard?"

She nodded. "I'd hoped…" She broke off when Gibson wrapped his arms around her, having placed the flamethrower on the ground.

"It's good to hope. Good to have faith that things will work out in the end." His arms tightened around her. "Did Zoe wake you? I told her to let you sleep longer."

She drew back to shake her head. "No. I don't know what woke me." Unless it was his sister glaring at her. "Are you okay?"

"Yeah." He drew back, keeping an arm around her. "Are you coming with us?" He nodded towards the vehicle, Haleb coming out the back doors without the freezing backpack.

"Yeah." Piper glanced at the flamethrower. "Why did you need that?"

"After freezing Freddie, we built a pyre with some of the plants we cut back yesterday." Gibson glanced at the stars. "Although it's probably after midnight by now, which means it was the day before. We used the smaller stuff."

"Oh." The thought of Freddie being burned on a

pyre made her feel uncomfortable. Was that what all of them had to look forward to?

"We couldn't leave his body lying around and none of the crematoriums will be working," Gibson said.

Haleb picked up the flamethrower. "Want this in the vehicle or back where we got it from?"

"Where we got it from," Gibson said.

Zoe joined them, dressed in her protective gear, as Haleb walked away. "Why aren't you dressed yet?" She looked Piper up and down. "Everyone needs to wear their protective gear when we leave the compound."

"My fault." Gibson kept his arm around Piper's shoulders.

Zoe glared at her brother. "You should know better." She turned to Piper. "Hurry up and get ready before your parents learn that we're taking you with us and I have to listen to another lecture." She pointed a finger at Piper. "They keep trying to treat me like a little kid and they will be kicked out." Zoe spun on her heel, striding towards the vehicle.

Chapter Twenty-Eight

Piper stared after Zoe. "My parents lectured her?"

Gibson chuckled. "So she said when she came looking for me earlier." He kept his arm around Piper's shoulders as he walked to the back of the vehicle with her. "I'm sure they'll learn. Zoe is pretty much the boss around here. Even Emerson doesn't argue with her."

Piper clambered into the back of the vehicle and picked up the protective gear that was folded neatly on one of the bench seats. "I don't blame him." She glanced towards the front of the vehicle where Zoe was putting information into the navigator on the dash, clearly ignoring them. "Who else is going with us?" She started putting on her protective gear.

"Only Haleb. We didn't want to invite Linda and risk your parents being a problem," Gibson said.

Piper grinned. "They would have been." Finished

putting on her protective gear, she sat on the seat, angled so she could face Gibson.

"It'll take us a couple of hours to get there." Gibson climbed in the back with Piper, closing the door before sitting beside her. "We're hoping it won't be as bad away from the city."

"Don't hold your breath." Zoe opened her door and leaned out slightly. "You're in the front with me."

Haleb walked around the front of the vehicle and climbed in. "You sure you don't want me to invite either of my brother-in-laws along?"

"No. We're going to need all the space we've got for passengers." Zoe started the vehicle and drove into the area between the two fences, waiting for one gate to close before she opened the other. "Piper is sure to find others she can't leave behind."

Gibson chuckled at his sister's dry tone, slipping an arm around Piper. "More than likely."

Piper didn't know if she should feel offended. "It's the right thing to do."

Zoe's answer was a snort.

Gibson tightened his hold on Piper, smiling when she looked in his direction.

She wished they didn't have to wear the breathing masks so that she could actually see his smile, not just the humour in his eyes and the crinkle to the side of them. "Do you think they'll be okay?"

Gibson shrugged. "I hope so." He paused a moment. "Try and get some more sleep. Who knows what we'll find."

She doubted she'd be able to sleep, but leaned against Gibson anyway, surprised to be gently shaken awake. "What time is it?" She automatically reached up to rub at her eyes, unable to do so with the breathing mask in the way.

"We're minutes away," Gibson said.

"It's nearly three. We had to take a few detours along the way," Zoe said.

Piper wasn't sure if she should ask why. The answer was likely to be extremely unpleasant after what she'd seen in the past few days.

"I can see the farmhouse ahead. With the amount of lights they've got on I doubt we'll have a friendly greeting," Haleb said.

"I don't blame them." Zoe slowed as they approached the farmhouse. "Gibson, sort out the temperature in here."

Gibson leaned into the front of the vehicle to adjust the temperature. "Might not want to get too close."

"I know what I'm doing." Zoe drove forward a few more metres before pulling up.

"Want me to go out there?" Haleb asked.

"I can," Gibson offered.

Zoe grabbed hold of her brother's arm when he started to move back. "Stop rushing into danger all the time."

"I'll go." Piper reached for the back door. "Is the temperature right yet?"

Gibson pulled away from Zoe to draw Piper to himself. "Not alone. I'll go with you."

"You better not get yourself killed," Zoe muttered. She reached for a gun. "Warn them I'll shoot if they harm you."

Gibson opened the back door and hopped out. He turned to help Piper.

She jumped out, not taking his hand until she was beside him. "How do we let them know we're not going to hurt them?" She doubted telling them Zoe was willing to shoot would achieve that goal.

"Freddie's daughter is called Olivia and she has an eight-year-old daughter called Harper and a five-year-old son called Asher."

"The one who thinks a dog is better than pie." Piper couldn't help smiling at the memory of Freddie's story.

"Yeah. Keep your hands where they can see them so they know we haven't got a weapon aimed at them." Gibson raised his hands before he stepped around the vehicle, hands open, palms faced forward. "We're looking for Olivia. We have a message from her father."

Piper followed, keeping her hands up. Away from the protection of the vehicle she felt vulnerable, wanting to look in every direction at once. She forced herself to keep her gaze on the house in front, not wanting to give the occupants the impression that they didn't trust them by continually scanning the area. She was certain Zoe was already keeping an eye on things. She wasn't about to let anything happen to her brother.

"How do we know you're who you say you are?" a man called out from inside the house.

Gibson continued to slowly walk forward. "How do we know Olivia is in there? Or if you've done something to her and her kids."

"Olivia is my fiancée. What's the message her father sends?"

"I want to hear Olivia speak first." Gibson stopped by the driver's side window.

Piper caught a glimpse of a face pressed against the far left window. A young boy, a girl joining him. She stopped beside Gibson, keeping her voice low. "Window on the far left."

"I see them."

"Something is wrong."

"I'm Olivia," a female voice called out. "What message did my father send? Is he safe?"

"How do we know you're who you say you are?" Gibson called out. "What is your father's name?"

"It's Freddie. How do I know you're who you say you are?" the woman demanded. "What are the names of my children?"

"Harper and Asher. What is the name of your father's dog?" Gibson asked.

Piper continued to watch the children. "Harper is using sign language. Spelling out the word 'help'. We have to do something."

"Whatever we do might get all of them killed," Gibson said.

Zoe wound down the window. "Get back in the vehicle and let's get out of here."

"It's Molly," the woman called out.

"That's it. We're going," Zoe said. "That was the name of Freddie's wife. She was shot during an armed robbery about a decade ago."

Gibson raised his voice. "Okay. You're Olivia. We'll take you to safety where we can catch up over apple pie." He emphasised the last word before lowering his voice, keeping his face towards the house.

"We can't leave them in there. We can rescue them. Have a bit of faith, Zoe. We can do this."

Piper eyed the distance between the window and the front door. "We'll bring the vehicle closer so you don't have to be out in the spores too long."

"We will not," Zoe said.

"Yes we will. Park against the house between the window and the door. Haleb can go in the window where the kids are. No one is in that room or they'd drag the kids away from the window," Piper said.

Zoe started the engine. "This is the worst plan ever."

Gibson slowly walked towards the house. "I've got medical masks I can give you to use before you come outside."

Piper walked beside him, glancing at the vehicle as Zoe drove in a large circle to get the vehicle in place.

"Give the medical masks to the smaller one. You stay back," the man called out.

Gibson stopped and faced Piper. "You don't have to do this."

"I know. But we can't leave them in there." She took the masks he drew from a sealed pocket, holding them out to her. When she would have stepped away, he wrapped his arms around her, drawing her close.

"The safety is on."

Before she could ask him what he meant, she felt something solid slipped into her back, sealed pocket. "I can't-"

"You will if you need to." Gibson drew away from her.

Piper slipped the medical masks into a sealed, front pocket. A glance towards the vehicle showed it was in place and Haleb was getting out the back door. She strode towards the front door, raising her hands. "We'll take all of you to safety. It's what Freddie asked of us."

"What makes you think your place is any safer than here? There's not a single plant around here," the man said.

"That'll change soon enough," Gibson said. "If it hasn't already."

Piper reached the front door, glancing towards the vehicle. Haleb was helping the kids out the window. Relief rushed through her. At least they were safe. "Are you going to let me in?"

"Tell the other one to move back further," the man said.

"I heard."

Piper glanced over her shoulder to see Gibson move both back and towards the left of the house. The sound of the door opening had her heart racing, her breath catching in her throat when it opened enough for her to see a gun pointed directly at her. She wanted to take a step back, but managed to remain still.

"Inside." The man moved out of the way. "And keep your hands where I can see them."

Chapter Twenty-Nine

Piper slowly entered the house, seeing another man held a gun to a woman's head. "What's going on?" She knew, but she didn't want them to realise.

"That's a kid. Why'd your father send a kid?" the second man demanded of Olivia.

"She's a neighbour," Olivia said. "Don't hurt her. She wouldn't hurt anyone."

"I take Molly for her daily walk. Or I used to," Piper said. "And her two pups. When she had them. I kept them safe." She glanced at Olivia, hoping she understood the message.

"I don't want those medical masks. I want the ones you and your friends are wearing," the first man said.

"We've got more in the vehicle," Piper said.

"You're going to tell your friends to come in here while my friend goes around the back and gets the vehicle," the first man said.

Piper nodded, even though she had no intention of doing that at all.

"How many of you are there?" the second man demanded.

"There are two with me." She was glad the windows of the vehicle were a dark tint.

"Right, both of you stand in front of me and don't try anything." The first man gestured Olivia and Piper to one side of the foyer. He pointed the gun at Olivia. "You try anything and I'll make your kids pay."

Piper reached for Olivia's hand when she was standing beside her, squeezing it tight.

"Give me about five minutes before you get the other one out of the vehicle. I'll need time to reach the corner." The second man strode towards the back of the house when the first one nodded.

The first man moved close to the window beside the door, twitching the curtain aside to glance out. He looked back at them. "Neither of you move."

"If I had a gun you'd be dead by now. My father taught me to shoot," Olivia said.

He glanced out the window again, chuckling. "Yeah, right. You against the two of us. Like you'd win that fight."

Piper hoped Olivia told the truth. She moved closer

to the woman, letting go of her hand and removing the gun from the sealed pocket. "There's two against you now."

"But you don't have a gun. I do." He grinned before glancing out the window again.

Piper slipped the gun into Olivia's hand, not looking at Olivia when the woman glanced at her. "It's going to take more than guns to survive Dawn. It'll take friends you can trust."

"I have that. Now tell your friend to get out of the vehicle." The man glanced out the window again.

The moment his attention was off her, Piper dived towards the floor and away from Olivia, yelling out to her friends. "One is coming down the side of the house closest to the vehicle." Hitting the floor she rolled to the side, the gun following her movements, all the time expecting to feel a bullet.

A gun rang out and the man shouted, dropping his weapon.

Piper came to her feet, darting forward to grab the dropped weapon and move back out of the way. She held it on him, heart racing and limbs trembling. "Open the front door, Olivia." She didn't want to walk between Olivia and the gun she had pointed at the man. That sounded like a really bad idea to her.

Outside were several gunshots. Olivia opened the

door, stepping back. "It's safe in here now." She glanced at Piper. "My kids-"

"They're safe. We had them out of the house before I came inside."

Zoe came in the front door. "What are we going to do with him and his mate?" She gestured towards the man with her gun.

"Tie them up and leave a knife for them," Olivia said. "Where are my kids?"

Before Zoe could answer, two children ran towards the door, trying to get past her, calling for their mum. Zoe glared at them. "Give her a chance to get outside. Now out of the way so she can come out."

Piper kept her gun and gaze on the man, relieved when Zoe also turned her attention to him. "We need rope."

"Haleb is organising that." Zoe came further inside. "We should shoot them. We'd probably be doing them a favour. Drowning in your own blood isn't a pleasant way to die."

"We're not going to shoot them." Gibson came in the front door with a length of rope.

It didn't take long to tie both the men to chairs in the kitchen, leaving Haleb to watch them while they helped Olivia and her children pack what they needed to take with them.

Piper placed the last of the items in the back of the vehicle, hopping out to join Zoe, Gibson and Olivia. The two children were sitting in the foyer, having been told not to move or they'd be grounded. Piper had tried not to smile at the familiar threat. "You'll need to travel in insulated bags. It'll be too cold in the vehicle for you."

"How many bags do you have?" Olivia asked.

"Five. And we call them body bags," Zoe said.

"That won't be enough." Olivia slowly shook her head.

"For you and two kids? That's plenty." Zoe crossed her arms over her chest. "We only came to get you."

Piper smiled when Olivia crossed her arms over her chest and met Zoe's glare with one of her own. "Who else do you need to take?"

"The neighbours. I've known most of them my entire life." Olivia made a sweeping motion with her hand to encompass the area. "We can't leave them behind."

"How many?" Zoe demanded.

"Thirty-two, no, it'd be thirty-three now. The neighbours over the rise have a new grandchild."

Zoe shook her head, about to speak.

"We can't leave them behind," Piper said.

Zoe turned her glare on Piper. "Yes, we can. I

already told you," she pointed a finger at Piper, "that you better not get–"

Piper interrupted. "I know. You don't have to keep telling me. But we're not leaving them behind."

"The compound isn't big enough for everyone," Zoe said.

"They can camp in the laneway," Gibson suggested.

"No. We need it as a safe area between us and the plants," Zoe said.

Piper turned to Olivia, leaving Gibson to argue with Zoe. "We won't fit everyone in. Have you got a vehicle?"

Olivia shook her head. "Neither do some of the neighbours. Or at least not enough vehicles to take all their family. There's the wagon Dad made for my wedding." She smiled wryly. "I had ideas of an old fashioned farm wedding with a horse drawn wagon filled with straw. You can't imagine exactly how much straw makes you itch and gets into everything." Her smile faded. "Should have taken it as an omen about how the marriage would end up and run while I could."

"Does the wagon work?" Piper asked. "And how will we tow it?"

"Dad fixed it up for the kids to enjoy, a couple

of years ago, and bought two horses for it." Olivia gestured towards the barn. "It's stored in there."

Gibson turned away from Zoe. "Sounds good. Where are the horses?"

"In the paddock behind the house. Take a couple of carrots from the fridge and they'll come running. You'll need a light. The spotlights at the back of the house don't reach that far," Olivia said.

Gibson nodded. "Zoe keep an eye on the vehicle. I'll let Haleb know what's happening and the three of us will get the horses and wagon."

"What are we going to do with a couple of horses?" Zoe demanded.

Gibson laughed softly. "Keep the grass in the laneway down?"

It took half an hour to get ready and on the road, the horse drawn wagon following the vehicle, Haleb choosing to go with Olivia and her children. A gun rested on his lap as he kept an eye on the surroundings, spotlights having been attached to the wagon so they could see what was around them. Olivia, the kids and the horses wore medical masks, the horses having been more accepting of the masks than Asher had been.

Piper looked out the window at the first farmhouse they approached, sitting alone in the back of the vehicle. She watched as Olivia drew the horses to a stop beside them and jumped off the wagon seat, heading towards the house, calling out to the occupants. A woman came running out, throwing her arms around Olivia.

By the time they'd visited all the neighbours, Olivia explained what was happening, waited for the neighbours to gather their gear and handed out medical masks, the sun was rising. The procession back to the compound was slow and people joined them along the way, some walking, others in various vehicles.

Zoe glared at the people following. "They won't fit. Only a handful will."

Gibson rested a hand on her shoulder. "We can't leave them behind."

"It's not going to help them," Zoe muttered.

"We don't know that. Besides, soon nowhere will be safe."

Zoe pulled up out the front of the compound. "They better not try and get in."

Gibson opened the door. "I'll sort everyone out. Have a bit of faith."

Piper followed him, not wanting to be left with Zoe and her mutters about getting them killed. She stood back while Gibson talked to Olivia, Haleb joining her. She turned to him. "Do you think they'll try and get in?"

Haleb shrugged. "I hope not. The laneway isn't big enough for this crowd."

Olivia nodded and turned away, Gibson striding back to them. "Tell Zoe to take the vehicle inside. We're about to let everyone know there isn't room for most of them." Gibson took hold of Piper's hand. "You can go inside too if you want."

She shook her head. "I'll stay out here with you." She had the weapon she'd taken from the farmhouse. Not that she knew how to use it or if she'd be able to use it.

Gibson momentarily tightened his grip on her hand before letting go and joining Olivia who was walking through the crowd, talking to people.

Haleb kept his weapon ready. "Don't worry. This lot don't look like they'll cause trouble."

"How do you know?"

"Because most of them appear to be in shock and willing to accept any hope, no matter how small."

She took a closer look at the people milling around, most of them looking like they didn't know what to do next. A smile slowly formed. "Zoe should be out here."

"What?" Haleb glanced at Piper.

She chuckled. "Zoe loves to throw around orders and tell people what to do."

Haleb chuckled too. "She does tend to get things done though."

Chapter Thirty

Piper slowly turned, taking in everything. The people gathered out the front of the compound, the scrubland behind them, the fence around the compound and behind the fence her parents. They watched the proceedings, clutching each others' hands. She half expected them to demand that she come inside. When they remained where they were, her gaze was drawn to Zoe, cleaning the vehicle before taking it into the compound.

"What's wrong?" Haleb asked.

"We need another compound. Actually, two compounds." She strode to the gate, catching Zoe's attention and beckoning her over.

Zoe left the vehicle in the compound and strode to the gate, carrying a gun. Once the inside gate was closed, she opened the outer gate, closing it behind her before joining Piper and Haleb. "What?"

Piper gestured towards the crowd. "This is what you should be doing. Organising everyone. Look at them. They need someone to tell them what needs to be done."

"Why do you think I know what needs to be done. I can't help them." Zoe crossed her arms over her chest. "You better not be thinking of letting them in the compound."

Piper shook her head. "No. We need more compounds and they can build them. You can organise them to gather supplies. Tell them what needs to be built."

"If you know what needs to be done, why don't you tell them?"

"Because that job wouldn't suit me."

"And what job would suit you?" Zoe demanded.

Piper's gaze was drawn first to her parents who continued to watch her and then to Olivia's children who remained on the wagon. "Finding the people for you to organise."

"Of course." Zoe's tone dripped heavily with sarcasm. "I should have known." She glared at Piper for a moment, then glanced at the crowd. "I guess someone needs to get them sorted. We can't have them camping at the front gate making it difficult for us to go out." Zoe strode to the wagon, vaulting onto the bed. "Okay, listen up. You can't remain at the front gate. There's a better location on the eastern side. And you need to gather supplies. If you don't want to be killed by Dawn then you're going to have to find the materials to create large enough barriers to keep the spores out."

"What type of materials?" a man called out from the crowd.

"Tools, metal or timber posts, fine mesh wire, solar panels, food." Zoe glanced around the crowd. "And probably chemical toilets or this area is going to become unliveable pretty quick."

Numerous questions were called out at once.

Zoe spoke over them, her voice louder than the handful that spoke. "One at a time. Try putting your hand up. We're meant to be civilised people. Act like it."

Gibson joined Piper and Haleb, humour in his voice. "Whose idea was it to get Zoe out there?"

Haleb chuckled, nodding his head towards Piper.

Gibson slipped an arm around her shoulders. "Good plan." He turned to Haleb. "Can you keep an eye on things out here? I'll collect medical masks and sort out which people are meant to be in the laneway. I should also show both of you the code to get inside."

"Do you want help handing out medical masks? And do we have enough?" Piper asked.

"We'll run out eventually. But not for a while. Dad ordered ten thousand. That should keep us going for a bit."

"Ten thousand?" Piper followed Gibson to the gate, watching as he keyed in both codes, hoping she remembered them.

"Yeah. He was determined to save the world. Or at least his little corner of it." Gibson nodded towards Tricia and Alistair. "Looks like your parents are waiting to talk to you."

Piper followed Gibson into the laneway, Haleb remaining outside, guarding Zoe. "Yeah. They've been waiting since we returned." She waited for all possible spores to be frozen before walking to the inner gate. Her gaze remained on her parents, trying to figure out if she was in trouble from their expressions.

Gibson opened the inner gate, removing his breathing mask once it was closed, grinning at her. "Everything will be okay. Have a little faith. If they try and stop you from going outside the gates we'll set Zoe on them."

Piper returned his grin. "Enough of a threat to

make anyone behave." She removed her breathing mask, her grin fading. "I better see what they want."

Gibson drew her close. "I heard what you did at Olivia's. She told me when I was helping her pack her gear." His lips brushed lightly across hers. "I'm glad you weren't hurt."

She watched as he walked to the laboratory, stunned. He'd kissed her? Although it had barely been a kiss. Seeing her parents start towards her, she ran after Gibson, reaching him before he entered the laboratory.

He turned to face her. "Is everything okay?"

She stared at him for a moment before she nodded. "Yeah. Be careful out there." She slid one arm around his neck, holding the breathing mask in her other hand. "I don't want you hurt either." Then she kissed him the way she'd wished he'd kissed her before.

Gibson returned her kiss, eventually drawing away with a grin. "I'm sure Zoe's got it under control." With another grin, he entered the laboratory.

Piper turned to face her parents, her grin fading as she strode towards them. Dread pooled in her stomach. Worse than what she'd felt when she'd faced a gun. She tried to convince herself that at least her parents didn't want to kill her. Not like some of the people she'd met in the past few days. She came to a stop in front of them, having no idea what to say.

"We talked to Emerson," Tricia said.

"Okay." They better not have arranged a different job for her. Not when she'd finally figured out which job was hers.

"He told us about Freddie. Said you were all Freddie could talk about before he died," Alistair said.

She glanced past her parents to the front gate. Later she'd tell Olivia to stop letting everyone know what she'd done at the house. Her parents would lock her away if they heard. "He didn't deserve to die. Not like that." She would talk to Olivia after someone else had told her about her father. She didn't want that task.

"We also talked to Caden and his family."

At her mum's words, Piper tried to think if she'd done anything crazy that time. Nothing came to mind. But someone had pointed a gun at her. "There was space in the compound for them." She shrugged.

"I don't like you going out there." Tricia turned as she gestured towards the front gate.

"I'm—"

Tricia interrupted Piper. "I'm not going to stop you. As much as I want to keep you in here, we can't. We're only here because you've been saving lives."

"You… I…" Piper closed her mouth, looking from

her mum to her dad. Surely she hadn't heard correctly. "What?"

Tricia smiled, closing the space between them to wrap her arms around Piper. "We're so proud of you. Terrified, but proud."

Alistair wrapped his arms around both of them. "We raised you to do what's right. We shouldn't complain when you follow what we taught you."

"I can keep going out of the compound?"

"Yes." Alistair let her go.

Tricia held on a moment longer before she let go too. "Don't take any unnecessary risks."

She really needed to have that chat with Olivia before her parents managed to. "Okay." She felt dazed. Her parents were not the sort to let her roam the countryside.

Alistair rested his hand on Piper's shoulder. "Do you know how it made me feel when I was told earlier today that my daughter is a hero?"

"Uhm, you were?" Obviously they hadn't been talking to Zoe.

Alistair chuckled. "Don't sound so surprised. What did you think people would say when you save their life?"

"Thank you?"

Tricia laughed softly. "Don't be so modest." She

glanced towards the laboratory when the door opened and Gibson stepped out with a bundle of medical masks. "We should let you go. I'm sure you've got work to do."

Piper glanced towards Gibson. "Ahh, yeah. Of course." She dredged up a smile she hoped didn't show any of the shock she was feeling. "I'll see you later." She took a step away from them.

"For dinner. Bring Gibson with you. We'd like to meet him," Alistair said.

"Uhm, okay." She glanced towards Gibson who strode towards the front gate. "I better go." When her parents nodded, both smiling, she ran after Gibson, catching him before he reached the gate. "Don't tell my parents what happened at Olivia's." She put on her breathing mask.

Gibson chuckled, putting on his mask too. "Did you get into trouble?"

"No."

"What did they want?"

She stepped into the laneway with Gibson. "To tell me I'm a hero."

"You sound shocked."

"I am."

Gibson chuckled again. "You shouldn't be. Look at

the way some are acting. They'd rather kill than save lives."

"Not everyone." She gestured towards the crowd out the front. "This lot don't look like they're about to shoot anyone."

"No, because they have hope. Right now Zoe has convinced them that if they work together and follow her orders there's a good chance they'll survive. They're expecting to be tested for infection and moved onto a more secure location if they're clear."

"What location?" Piper asked.

"Zoe told them that the healthy ones would be sent to build in safe zones with more joining them."

It took her a few seconds to realise what he meant. "The Snowy Mountains."

Gibson nodded. "There's areas that are untouched. National Forests. Some of the camping grounds can be improved and made into permanent places to live. Areas that don't get above fifteen degrees Celsius during summer and that snow in winter."

"Who came up with that idea?"

"Zoe."

Piper grinned. "I knew she was the right one to get them organised."

With another chuckle, Gibson slipped an arm

around her shoulders. "Let's get these masks handed out while Zoe continues to do her thing."

"Oh, my parents want to meet you. You're invited to dinner."

Gibson opened the outer gate. "Sounds good. By the time we finish out here none of us are going to be interested in cooking. Think they'll mind if Zoe joins us?"

Piper grinned. Zoe would be the perfect person to deflect some of her parents' interest in Gibson. "I'm sure they won't mind." Not that it would matter if they did. Her parents wouldn't say anything until Gibson and Zoe left. She stepped outside the compound, taking the medical masks Gibson handed her.

"Want to split up or stay together while we hand them out?"

She scanned the crowd. No one looked menacing. "Together." She smiled up at him, wondering if he could see the smile in her eyes, like she could see one in his.

Chapter Thirty-One

Piper walked through the compound, side stepping a child who ran across her path. She smiled. The place had certainly changed in the past two and a half weeks. There were more people in the compound for starters. Which was why it was often difficult to find Zoe lately. She hadn't seen her since Selene's seventeenth birthday dinner last night. Zoe had grudgingly attended, but Piper was pretty certain the girl had enjoyed herself.

She returned to Zoe's cottage, knocking on the door again. No one answered. Breathing out heavily, she turned slowly, scanning the area. There was nowhere else to look. She'd searched the entire compound.

Gibson strode towards Piper, stopping beside her with a grin. "Did you find her?"

Piper was about to say 'no' when she spotted Pie

curled up at the corner of the cottage. Zoe couldn't be far away. The dog never let Zoe out of her sight. Another glance around showed nothing. Her jaw dropped. There was one place she hadn't looked. Taking several steps away from the cottage, she looked up.

Zoe peered over the edge, glaring at Piper when their gazes collided. She shook her head, pressing a finger to her lips.

Gibson moved to where Piper stood, looking up. He chuckled. "I didn't take you for a coward."

"We're enjoying the sun," Zoe stated.

Haleb sat up, far enough from the edge that he hadn't been noticeable while lying down. "Apparently it's a lovely day." He grinned, glancing at Zoe who sent her glare towards him.

"It is a lovely day." Zoe looked towards Piper and Gibson again. "Or at least it was before I was interrupted."

Piper looked from Zoe to Haleb and back to Zoe again, not at all surprised to find him nearby. He'd become Zoe's bodyguard, stepping into the roll effortlessly. Refusing to let her go anywhere alone. "The convoy is ready to go."

"They're not taking Pie. She's mine. Freddie asked me to look after her," Zoe said.

"Harper and Asher miss their grandfather. Pie is all they have left of him," Piper said.

"No. She's mine." Zoe swung off the edge of the roof, landing lightly on the ground, Haleb landing beside her. She pointed a finger at Piper. "Mine."

Piper shrugged. She'd tried. That was all she could do. Olivia couldn't expect any more of her than that. "Okay."

"Time to see everyone off," Gibson said. "Gear up and we'll meet you at the front gate."

"You better not keep me waiting." Zoe strode inside, Pie and Haleb following her.

Gibson slipped an arm around Piper's shoulders. "I don't think Olivia expected you to have any luck, but she couldn't leave without trying one more time." He walked towards his cottage, keeping his arm around Piper's shoulders.

"I suppose not." She glanced towards the front gates, seeing the assorted vehicles parked out the front, people gathered around them wearing medical masks, some wearing protective gear. Her parents, Caden and Linda wore protective gear.

Gibson opened the front door of his cottage, his gaze drawn to where Piper glanced. "You can change your mind."

Shaking her head, she stepped inside. "No. My

place is here." Picking up the protective gear folded neatly on the lounge chair, she began to pull it on. "And the new village is where my parents belong. It's not like I won't ever see them again. They'll be back when the village is established." She had no idea how long that would take.

Gibson's grin was mostly hidden when he pulled on the breathing mask. It couldn't hide the humour in his eyes. "I've never met anyone so passionate about the environment and pollution as your dad."

Piper smiled wryly. "Sorry about last night." She hadn't immediately realised her dad had cornered Gibson to talk on his favourite subjects. When she'd noticed, he'd had a look of desperation in his eyes and had appeared to be looking for a way to escape.

"That's okay. At least we know your dad will make sure the new village is ecologically sound and fits in with the surrounding trees of the National Forest." Gibson led the way outside.

Piper tried not to sigh when she noticed Zoe and Haleb were already at the gate waiting for them. Pie was nowhere in sight. She looked past Zoe, and the gathered vehicles in front of the compound, to the fenced area where vegetables had recently been planted. Like the compound, the fine mesh was kept at a freezing temperature, the water for the plants frozen before taken inside.   Beyond that structure, barely visible from where she stood, were countless Dawn stretching towards them. The plants had grown at a phenomenal rate, devouring buildings and synthetic structures along the way.

"I told you not to keep me waiting." Zoe crossed her arms over her chest when they reached her.

"Time to see everyone off." Gibson opened the gate, stepping into the laneway.

Piper joined him, her gaze drawn to the four horses now in the laneway. There were no longer people staying in the laneway. Two compounds had been built for them to stay in. There were a couple of timber buildings but most of them were living in canvas tents.

Gibson took hold of Piper's hand. "Are you sure you're okay? You're very quiet."

Zoe opened the outer gate the moment the inner one was closed. "She should be celebrating. Considering her parents said they weren't going to stop her going out to rescue people, they interrogate her long enough each time she does."

Piper grinned, after glancing towards her parents to make sure they wouldn't have heard Zoe's comments. Her attention was caught by Selene and Wyatt walking towards her. She met her friend halfway. "Should you be out here?" Neither of them wore protective clothing or medical masks. The only good part about being infected by Dawn was that you couldn't be reinfected.

"Don't fuss," Selene said. "My grandparents are bad enough."

She took Selene's hand, squeezing lightly, hearing in her friend's voice that she wasn't really annoyed by the fussing. "I need to say goodbye to my parents." She looked to Gibson who nodded, and Zoe who shook her head. She grinned. "Come on, Zoe. I'm sure they'll have last minute questions."

"More like last minute orders," Zoe muttered. But she followed Piper to her parents, who were standing with Linda, Caden and those organised to guard the group. They also had permanent guards who protected the compound from people who tried to force their way in. Olivia was further away, trying to calm her children. She'd chosen to travel to the village they planned to build so they wouldn't be without medical help, declining Emerson's request to remain and help him find not only a prevention, but also a safe method of curing people. He still hoped to find a way to use the toddler's natural immunity to create a vaccine.

Gibson clapped his sister on the shoulder. "Don't

worry, Zoe. I'm sure they'll get those new communication towers up along the way and will be able to contact us any time they have questions to ask." Any synthetic parts on the new towers were covered by natural materials so Dawn couldn't destroy any of the necessary components.

Tricia and Alistair came forward to crush Piper to them, giving her last minute instructions and asking once more if she was certain she wanted to remain at the compound. Tricia had a sheen of moisture in her eyes.

"Mum." Piper drew out the word, pulling away from her parents. "I'll be fine. You'll be too busy to miss me."

Linda stepped forward. "Don't worry, Tricia. Caden and I will head back to the compound, with half the guards, the moment you lot get settled. We'll keep an eye on Piper for you while you're gone."

Piper nearly groaned. "I don't need anyone to keep an eye on me."

Caden joined them, winking when he caught Piper's gaze. "We'll take good care of your daughter, Tricia."

Piper looked from her parents to Linda and Caden. So much for being some great hero. It didn't seem that way with the way everyone treated her. "You need to get on the road if you want to make it to your first destination before dark." They would camp overnight at each location where communication towers needed to be erected. "You two are the ones who need to be careful."

There were some more instructions, her parents hugged her a couple of times and Olivia finally got her kids to settle down and came to ask Zoe about Pie. The answer was a glare and Zoe crossing her arms over her chest.

Piper stood between Gibson and Selene as she waved goodbye to her parents. She tried to ignore the touch of fear she felt as the vehicles headed out of sight. They'd be fine. They had more than enough guards they could trust and people who were willing to fight to protect the village they planned to build at a National Forest campsite in the Snowy Mountains.

Selene slipped her hand in Piper's. "Remember the day we brought Dawn home?"

How could she forget a single moment of it? "Yeah." She glanced at Gibson with a smile when he took hold of her other hand.

"Remember our quote?" Selene asked.

That was yet one more thing she wouldn't be able to easily forget. "I really hope we don't end up with an endless Dawn."

"Neither do I." Selene's voice lowered. "But I wake up sometimes from nightmares that the world is covered in Dawn and there's no room left for us."

"That's not going to happen." Piper squeezed Selene's hand.

"We won't give up," Gibson said. "Someday we'll take our planet back and Dawn will be a mistake of the past."

She leaned against Gibson, continuing to hold Selene's hand. "Yes. We'll find a way to take back what's ours." Somehow. Past the farm compound delicate flowers bloomed, dandelion like fluff floating on the air. It would take more than a wish to destroy the invader they'd once welcomed to their world. But like Gibson had said, they weren't about to give up. "Dawn's time will eventually come to an end and we'll rebuild." Hopefully wiser and having learned something from their mistake, but like Zoe regularly pointed out, the only lesson most humans would probably learn was not to give up. But that was a start. It had kept humanity going this long and would hopefully keep it going a little longer.

Gibson squeezed her hand, smiling when she looked at him.

She returned his smile. It would be enough. They'd make sure it was.

Free Ebook

Subscribe to Avril's newsletter and receive a free ebook. This ebook is exclusive to those on her mailing list. To find out more about this offer visit: www.avrilsabine.com/free-ebook

*

We value your privacy and will not sell, rent, exchange or loan your email address to third parties. Your information is confidential and you are under no obligation to remain on the mailing list and can unsubscribe at any time.

Acknowledgements

Thanks to the usual crew and a special thanks to Lloyd for going over all the science in the book. If there are any mistakes, they're mine.

To The Reader

If you enjoyed this book, why not consider leaving a review to help other readers discover it too? Reader engagement is one of the few ways that lets an author know readers want more books in a particular series or genre. So leave a review and tell friends, not only about this book but also about other ones you've enjoyed, so you can continue to enjoy books by your favourite authors for years to come.

Dreams are meant to be lived,

Avril.

About The Author

Avril is an Australian author who lives with her family on acreage in South East Queensland. She writes mostly young adult and children's speculative fiction, but has been known to dabble in other genres. You can find more information about her at www.avrilsabine.com where you can also subscribe to her newsletter to be kept informed about new releases, current projects, blog posts and exclusive news.

Titles By Avril Sabine

Stories about strong characters and characters who discover their strengths.

SERIES

Assassins Of The Dead- Young Adult Fantasy/ Paranormal

Book 1: Dark Blade

Book 2: Dragon Touched

Book 3: Society Against Vampires

Book 4: King's Request

Dragon Blood- Young Adult Urban Fantasy (with elements of romance)

(5 book series)

Book 1: Pliethin

Book 2: Wyvern

Book 3: Surety

Book 4: Knight

Book 5: Mage

Dragon Mage- Young Adult Urban Fantasy (with elements of romance)

(Series two of Dragon Blood series)

Book 1: Promise

Dragon Blood Chronicles- Young Adult Urban Fantasy (with elements of romance)

(Companion stand alone series to Dragon Blood)

Book 1: Oath

Book 2: Betrayed

Guardians Of The Round Table- Young Adult Fantasy LitRPG

(Co-written with Storm and Rhys Petersen)

Book 1: Dexterity Fail

Book 2: Goblin Boots

Book 3: Singed Feathers

Book 4: Frog Mage

Book 5: Crystal Mine

Book 6: Cursed Harp

Rosie's Rangers- Young Adult Western Steampunk

(6 book series)

Book 1: Justice

Book 2: Vengeance

Book 3: Treachery

Book 4: Accused

Book 5: Wanted

Book 6: Corruption

Mark Of Kings- Children's Fantasy

(Upper middle grade/preteen)

(4 book series)

Book 1: The Arena

Book 2: The Island

Book 3: The Assassin

Book 4: The King

STAND ALONE SERIES

Demon Hunters- Young Adult Urban Fantasy/ Horror (with elements of romance)

Book 1: Blood Sacrifice

Book 2: Retribution

Book 3: Tainted

Book 4: Premonition

Book 5: Cursed

Book 6: Feud

Book 7: Extrication

Plea Of The Damned- Young Adult Urban Fantasy/Paranormal

(6 book series)

Book 1: Forgive Me Lucy

Book 2: Forgive Me Aiden

Book 3: Forgive Me Jena

Book 4: Forgive Me Kobe

Book 5: Forgive Me Marti

Book 6: Forgive Me Dawson

Realms Of The Fae- Young Adult Urban Fantasy (with elements of romance)

The Sword (short story in Like A Girl Anthology)

Heart Of Stone

Book 1: A Debt Owed

Book 2: Marked By The Hunt

Book 3: The Magic Collector

Book 4: An Unexpected Betrayal

Book 5: Imprisoned By Iron

Fairytales Retold (Short Stories)

Snow-White And Rose-Red

The Twelve Brothers

The Light Princess

Beauty And The Beast

Sleeping Beauty

Aschenputtel

The Golden Bird

The Frog Prince

The Death Of Koshchei The Deathless

Myths And Legends Retold (Short Stories)

Ion, Son Of Apollo

Sir Gawain And The Maid With The Narrow Sleeves

Princess Ilse, The Giant's Daughter

YOUNG ADULT NOVELS

Young Adult Fantasy (with elements of romance)

Elf Sight

Earth Bound

Young Adult Urban Fantasy

Stone Warrior (with elements of romance)

The Jungle Inside

Young Adult Contemporary (with elements of romance)

Through Your Eyes

The Ugly Stepsister

Perfect Little Princess

Young Adult Contemporary/Paranormal

Whispers In The Dark (with elements of romance and same sex relationships)

Over Too Soon (with elements of romance)

Young Adult Sci-Fi

Experiment X-One-Six (Urban Sci-Fi/Superheroes)

An Endless Dawn (Post Apocalyptic Sci-Fi)

CHILDREN'S BOOKS

Dragon Lord (Preteen/early teens) (Fantasy)

The Irish Wizard (Upper middle grade) (Urban Fantasy)

SHORT STORIES

Urban Fantasy

Eternally Late

Dealings With Joe

Glimpses (short story in That Moment When Anthology)

Contemporary

The Brat Next Door

Fantasy LitRPG

(Set in the same world as Guardians Of The Round Table Series)

Tales Of Inadon 1: The Disc (Co-written with Storm and Rhys Petersen) (short story in Game On! Anthology)

Post Apocalyptic Sci-Fi

Compulsive Directive

NONFICTION

A Year Of Weekly Writing Exercises (Creative Writing)

Cooking For Families With Allergies (Cooking) (Co-written with Storm Petersen)

Tell Me A Story, Grandma (Memoir)

For the most up to date details on available titles visit:

www.avrilsabine.com/books/bibliography

Disclaimer

This is a work of fiction. Names, characters, businesses, places, events and incidents are either the products of the author's imagination or used in a fictitious manner. Any resemblance to actual persons, living or dead, or actual events is purely coincidental. The opinions expressed or beliefs held are those of the characters and should not be assumed to be the opinions or beliefs of the author.